"Why have you come here?" Abbie demanded.

"I came here because I learned that someone from England was making inquiries about me," Sam told her promptly, "and as for what I want, I don't think it would be a very good idea if I answered that question right now. You aren't in the mood to hear what I want to say."

"I'll never be in the right mood to listen to anything you have to say other than 'goodbye'," Abbie told him bitterly. "And I've already heard you say that."

"No, Abbie, you haven't," he corrected her. "*You* were the one who said goodbye to me."

Abbie stared at him.

"Because you'd accused me of trying to pass another man's child off as yours...."

Dear Reader,

Welcome to

Everyone has special occasions in their life—times of celebration and excitement. Maybe it's a romantic event—an engagement or a wedding—or perhaps a wonderful family occasion, such as the birth of a baby. Or even a personal milestone—a thirtieth or fortieth birthday!

These are all important times in our lives and in THE BIG EVENT! you can see how different couples react to these events. Whatever the occasion, romance and drama are guaranteed!

We've been featuring some terrific stories from some of your favorite authors. If you've enjoyed this miniseries in Harlequin Romance®, we hope you'll continue to look out for THE BIG EVENT! in Harlequin Presents®. This month, we're delighted to bring you **Marriage Make Up** by Penny Jordan. In November, we have Sally Wentworth's intriguing **Runaway Fiancée.** Find out what happens when husband-to-be, Milo Caine, tracks down the woman who ran away from the wedding of the year!

Happy reading!

The Editors

PENNY JORDAN

Marriage Make Up

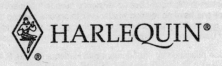

HARLEQUIN®

TORONTO • NEW YORK • LONDON
AMSTERDAM • PARIS • SYDNEY • HAMBURG
STOCKHOLM • ATHENS • TOKYO • MILAN • MADRID
PRAGUE • WARSAW • BUDAPEST • AUCKLAND

ISBN 0-373-11983-6

MARRIAGE MAKE UP

First North American Publication 1998.

Copyright © 1998 by Penny Jordan.

CHAPTER ONE

'MUM...'

Abbie Howard frowned as her twenty-two-year-old daughter's slightly hesitant voice interrupted her concentration on the accounts on which she was working. She had promised her accountants she would let them have them by the end of the week, but so much had happened since her daughter and her boyfriend had announced their engagement the previous weekend that she was now rather behind. Not that she minded Cathy interrupting her; the two of them had always had a very close relationship and everyone knew how much her daughter meant to her—too much, some people were occasionally inclined to say.

'You're not going to believe this,' Cathy informed her, perching on the edge of her mother's desk, swinging her long leg, which was still brown from her summer holidays.

People often remarked on how very dissimilar in looks mother and daughter were. Abbie was small, barely five feet two, and very fragile-looking, with delicate bones and an air of vulnerability about her that drew men to her like bees to honey—only for them to be both astonished and then huffily offended as she made it plain that playing the helpless little woman to their big strong man was the last thing she needed or wanted.

Her straight silky hair was naturally blonde, her eyes a deep and mesmerising blue-green, and at forty-three she could easily, had she wished to do so, have laid claim to being no older than a mere thirty-three and have been believed—not just by the male sex but by her own as well.

Not that she was likely to do any such thing. Abbie had no inhibitions about being open about her age, nor about the fact that she had a grown-up daughter.

Cathy, on the other hand, whilst she possessed her mother's entrancing blue-green eyes, was tall, with long bones and a mane of wild, tumbling deep brunette curls. As a child she had been inclined to be clumsy, and had even gone through a stage of secretly wishing she were more like her mother, of almost hating her own taller, stronger body, until Abbie had guessed what was happening and very quickly put a stop to it, making sure that her daughter, instead of rejecting her body shape, came to appreciate it.

'But I look just like Dad...you said so yourself when you showed me his photograph.' She *had* said so, Abbie remembered, and she also remembered how upset she had been when Cathy had told her that she didn't think she had ever had a daddy because she had never seen a picture of him. Abbie had shown her then the few photographs she had of Sam which she had not destroyed, hating having to look at them herself because of all the memories they brought back, all the pain.

Cathy had protested further. 'And he was horrible and you hate him...'

'But you aren't horrible and I don't hate you,' Abbie had comforted her, hugging and kissing her. 'I love you, and even though you have inherited your father's bone structure and colouring you're still your own person, Cathy, and I promise you that when you grow up you're going to love being so tall and elegant.'

'But at school they call me beanpole and beanie,' Cathy had wept.

'When I was at school they called me tiny,' Abbie

had told her. 'But it doesn't matter what other people say or think, my darling. What matters is what you think, and I promise you that when you grow up you are going to be very glad that you are *you*...'

And her mother had been right. Cathy was now the first person to acknowledge that. Just as she was always right...well, almost always. There were some things...

Hastily Cathy dismissed the disloyal thought she could feel forming. How was her mother going to take what she had to say to her? She had been marvellous when she and Stuart had told her about their engagement, insisting only that she be allowed to indulge herself as befitted the prospective mother of the bride.

Stuart had been more than willing to agree. He himself came from a large family and was comfortable with the idea of a large wedding.

And, despite the unhappiness and trauma of her own marriage, her mother had never tried to put her off getting married herself, Cathy acknowledged. Not that it would have done much good. She had fallen in love with Stuart virtually the moment she had seen him, and he with her, so he had told her later.

'What's wrong?' Abbie asked her daughter, pushing away her papers and turning to look up at her.

'I know you're not going to believe this,' Cathy responded nervously. 'But...I think...I think...' She looked down and started fidgeting with the laces on her boots. 'I think I...'

'Yes, go on...you think what?' Abbie encouraged her wryly.

'I think I saw Dad today...'

As she finished speaking she looked up warily to meet her mother's eyes.

The shock was rather like believing you were crossing a completely empty road and then suddenly realising there was a ten-ton truck bearing down on you at high speed, Abbie recognised, and she felt her body's adrenalin system surge to fight off the blow she had just been dealt.

'You're right,' she agreed flatly, when she thought she had her voice under control. 'I don't believe you. Cathy, It's impossible for your father to be here,' she added more gently, when she saw her daughter turn her head away and bite her lip. 'Your father is in Australia. He emigrated there just after...just after you were born, and there's no reason—' She stopped.

But Cathy picked up her unfinished sentence for her and supplied harshly, 'There's no reason for what? No reason for him to come back? No reason for him to want to see *me*...to know *me*...?'

Abbie could feel the lump forming in her throat. It hurt her unbearably that she who had learned to be so tough and protective of her child, who had thought she had done so well in making herself independent, in supporting them both, in giving her precious little girl all the love and security she could, had still somehow failed her.

She knew what it was, of course. Now that Cathy and Stuart were planning to get married, now that she had seen at first hand how Stuart's happily married parents related to one another, now that she was no doubt thinking of the future, and the children she would have herself, her natural curiosity about her father had risen to the surface of her consciousness. It was making her more curious about him, making her want to know more about him and no doubt making her wish that he felt the same way about her.

When Cathy had still been a small baby, Abbie had made a vow that she would always be honest with her about her father, that she would never lie to her about him or what he had done, but that at the same time she would do her best to protect her from the hurt she was bound to suffer once she was old enough to understand the truth.

And she had stuck by that vow, even though at times it had been very hard, and of course the older Cathy had got, the more aware, the harder it had been to protect her from what Abbie knew her daughter's own intelligence and emotions must tell her about her father.

How could *she*...how could *anyone* protect a child from the pain of knowing that its father didn't want it? She had done her best to make it up to Cathy, and she had been so proud when people commented on how well adjusted, how happy her daughter always seemed, but now she was wondering if she had congratulated herself too soon.

Because of that, because of her fear that she might not have been enough, that Cathy might still yearn for the father she had never had, she was less understanding and gentle with her than she might otherwise have been, telling her almost harshly, 'Forget about your father, Cathy. He doesn't have any place in your life. He never has had. I understand how you feel, but—'

'No, you don't. How can you?' Cathy interrupted her passionately. 'How can you understand?' she repeated, tears filling her eyes. 'Gran and Gramps love *you*. Gramps never, ever turned round and told Gran that *you* weren't his child, that he didn't want *you*... You never went to school and listened to all the other children talking about their fathers. You didn't have to walk down the aisle without—' Cathy broke off and whispered apologetically, 'I'm sorry, Mum... I didn't mean... I know it's not your fault...it's just...'

Abbie slid off her chair. With Cathy perched on her desk and her standing on her feet they were almost the same height. She wrapped her arms around her daughter, holding her close, comforting her just as she had done when she was a little girl, and for what felt like the hundred-millionth time she silently cursed the man who had brought them so much unhappiness.

Sam come back…? He wouldn't dare… Not after what he had done. She had made it more than plain to him the last time she'd seen him that henceforward she wanted nothing more to do with him, that he could keep his name, his money, his house and every other damn thing he had ever given her…except for his child. The child he had refused to accept could be his, the child she was claiming for herself and whom she would never, ever allow him to see again.

He had accused her of having sex with someone else, of conceiving her child with another man; had even had the gall to blame poor Lloyd. Lloyd, who would never…

He had started to say something else to her but she hadn't let him finish, pushing past him and preparing to walk out of the house she had shared with him for such a brief period of time.

That had been just after she had learnt she was pregnant, and she hadn't seen him since.

Abbie gave a pleased smile as she totted up the final column of figures some time later and closed the account book, placing it on top of the pile of other papers she had prepared for her accountants.

She knew how dubious several of her friends had been all those years ago—ten years ago—when she had announced that she was going to set up her own employment agency, but after fifteen years of experience of working in the hotel and catering trade, doing everything from waitressing and chambermaiding right through to being asked to take responsibility for organising a conference, she had learned enough to take such a big step and, more importantly, in her mind at least, she had the contacts on both sides of the business to succeed.

And she had been proved right; some of the staff who had been with her at the very start were still on her books. Her reputation had been passed by word of mouth to others. Along with her honesty and her loyalty to her staff, she was known never to supply staff to anyone she felt would abuse their position of authority over them in any way.

Her rates of pay were good and she explained firmly to anyone who quibbled about the amount she charged that she supplied the best and paid them accordingly. Abbie could supply catering staff right across the range, from a butler to lend *gravitas* to a formal private affair to a French chef to step in at the last minute and provide a buffet for five hundred people at an important convention, and everything in between.

Cathy, just as soon as she herself had been old enough, had been encouraged to earn her own extra pocket money by waiting at tables and serving behind a bar, just as her mother had once done. It didn't matter that once her daughter was at university Abbie could quite easily have afforded to supplement her grant very generously indeed; she'd wanted Cathy to have the independence and pride of knowing she could earn something for herself—just so long as her part-time work didn't detract from her studies, of course.

Abbie's own parents had offered to help her when her marriage had fallen apart, and had even begged her to move back home with them, but she had stubbornly insisted on supporting herself and now she was glad that she had done so, that she had made an independent life for herself here in this middle-sized, middle England town, where Sam had brought her as a new bride. Then they had both planned to make their future here—Sam as a university lecturer, with plans to become a writer one day, and Abbie also working at the university, in the archive department.

She glanced at her watch. Abbie had promised a friend who had become an aficionado of car-boot sales that she would go through her attic and see if she could find anything she wanted to dispose of. She had just enough time, if she was quick, to do so before her evening appointment with the manager of the new luxurious conference centre which had recently been opened as an extension of a local hotel.

Abbie herself had actually been approached to see if she would be interested in taking up the appointment as manager of the centre, but she had declined. She preferred being her own boss, being in charge of her own life. It might sometimes be lonelier that way, but it was also much safer—and safety when it came to her relationships, be they professional or personal, was something that was very, very important to her.

Not even her closest women-friends were allowed to get too close to her, just in case they might hurt her in some way, and as for men…

It wasn't that she was a man-hater, she denied as she made her way up the narrow flight of steps that gave her access to the attic space, no matter what some men might think. It was just that having been hurt very badly once, having been called a liar and worse, she was not about to give any man the opportunity to do so a second time. Why should she? She would be a fool if she did. That didn't mean there hadn't been times…*men* who had tempted her, but the memory of the pain Sam had caused her had always held her back. He had told her he loved her, that he would always love her, that he would never hurt her, but he had lied to her and she had believed him. How could she allow herself to trust another man after that? And not just for her own sake, for her own protection, but for Cathy's as well. Letting herself be hurt was one thing—she was an adult capable of making her own choices and of paying the price for them—but Cathy was more at risk. Cathy needed love and security.

Abbie pushed open the loft door, wrinkling her nose against the smell of stale air and dust. She hadn't been up here since just after Cathy had left home for university.

That was where Cathy had met Stuart, who had been taking a postgraduate course, and for a while, during the early stages of their relationship, Abbie had been worried that history was going to repeat itself.

It had been Fran, one of her oldest friends, who had warned her that she was in danger of alienating Cathy and damaging their relationship by becoming almost fixated on the belief that Stuart would hurt Cathy as Sam had hurt her.

'Stuart isn't the same,' Fran had told her, ignoring Abbie's refusal to discuss the subject with her. 'And even if he was,' she had added hardly, 'it's Cathy's right to make her own mistakes and her own choices. Sometimes the hardest thing about being a parent is letting go,' she had added wisely. 'I understand how you feel about Cathy, we all do, but she's an adult now, Abbie, and she's in love—'

'She *thinks* she's in love,' Abbie had interrupted angrily. 'She's only known him a matter of months, and already she's talking about moving in with him and—'

'Give her a chance,' Fran had counselled her. 'Give *them* a chance.'

'It's all right for you,' Abbie had grumbled. 'Your two are still only teenagers…'

'And you think that makes things easier?' Fran had rolled her eyes theatrically.

'Lloyd and Susie haven't been speaking all week. Lloyd caught her in a passionate embrace on the front doorstep the other night, and, predictably, he's suddenly turned into a protective, outraged father. And, of course, Susie's just at that age where she thinks she's old enough to make her own decisions—even though she isn't—and then she had to go and make matters worse by telling Lloyd that *she* was the one who snogged Luke, and not the other way round.'

'Hmm…' Momentarily Abbie had been diverted from her own problems.

Susie, Lloyd and Fran's elder daughter, was her god-child and back then had been a formidably feisty four-teen-year-old.

Along with Michelle, Fran and Lloyd's younger daughter, she had inherited her father's striking red hair and there was certainly no way that there was any remote resemblance between Lloyd's two daughters and her own, Cathy; if Sam had stayed around long enough he would very quickly have been forced to withdraw his accusation that Lloyd was Cathy's father.

Poor Lloyd. He hadn't met Fran when she and Sam had split up, and he had been wonderfully supportive in the early months when she had first been on her own, even hesitantly suggesting that perhaps they should marry. She had refused him, of course. She had known that she didn't love him, nor he her, even if everyone else had considered them to be a pair before Sam had appeared in her life.

Gingerly kneeling down in the only space she could find in the piles of stuff heaped all over the loft floor, Abbie started moving things out of the way so that she could get to the boxes of bits and pieces she knew were stored up there, and which she intended to hand on to her friend for her car-booting sorties.

As she did so she knocked over a pile of children's books. She paused to straighten them up, her eyes misting unexpectedly with tears as she recognised Cathy's first proper reading books.

How well she remembered the thrill of wonder and excitement she had felt when Cathy read her first proper word, her first full sentence. How proud she had been, how sure that her daughter was the cleverest, prettiest little girl there ever was, how humbled by the knowledge that she had given birth to this special, magical little person—the same special, magical, perfect child who had refused to eat her supper and later thrown a tantrum in the supermarket of blush-making proportions!

Abbie's smile faded as she also remembered how it had felt to have no one to share the special moments with, to have to wait until she could telephone her parents to tell them of Cathy's wondrous achievement.

Firmly she resisted the temptation to indulge in nostalgia. She was a busy career woman with a full diary and very little time; the daydreamer who went soft-eyed and emotional over every small incident in her life had been firmly suppressed and controlled. Another Abbie had had to develop and take shape. An Abbie whom people respected and sometimes even found slightly formidable, an Abbie who had learned to deal with life and all its small and manifold problems by and for herself... An Abbie who could and would, if necessary, fight like a tigress to protect her child, an Abbie who had no need of sentiment or regrets about the past, and who had certainly no need for a man in her life to mistrust her and hurt her.

She crawled across the floor to where she thought the boxes were stored, cursing as the dust made her cough and then cursing again and trying to ignore the ominous pattering and scuffling sounds she could hear in the rafters above her. Birds, that was all...nothing to worry about.

She reached the boxes and pulled the first one out, reaching for the one behind it. Only it wouldn't move; it appeared to be wedged against something. Gritting her teeth, Abbie felt behind it and then froze as her fingers curled round a piece of net fabric.

She knew immediately what it was, but, even though caution warned her to leave well alone and ignore it, for some reason she didn't.

Instead... Instead, her fingers trembled as she tugged harder on the fabric, clenching her teeth as she heard it rip slightly and the balled-up grey-white bundle of fabric finally came free of the small space she had jammed it into.

Once it had been pristine white, the tiny crystals sewn onto it glittering just as much as the diamonds in her engagement ring as she'd pirouetted around the fitting room, turning this way and that, her face flushed a delicate, happy pink as she waited for her mother to admire it.

She had been a fairy-tale bride, or so the report in the local paper had said, her wedding dress every little girl's dream and most big girls' as well—at least in those days. She had felt like a princess—a queen—as she'd walked proudly down the aisle on her father's arm. And when Sam had finally raised her veil after the vicar had married them, and she had seen the look in his eyes, she had felt as if...as though... She had felt immortal, she remembered. Adored, cherished...loved... And it had never even occurred to her that there might come a day when she would feel any different, when Sam wouldn't continue to look at her with that mixture of adoration and desire.

How naive she had been... How...how stupid.

Her mother, her parents, had tried to warn her that she was rushing into marriage, that she and Sam barely knew one another, but she wouldn't listen to them. They were old; they had forgotten what it was like to be in love, how it felt to be wanted, to want to be with that one special person so much that you actually hurt when they weren't there.

She and Sam had met by accident...literally... She had been riding her bicycle illegally through a part of the university campus which was prohibited to students, taking a short cut to a lecture.

At first when she had cannoned into Sam, almost running him down, she had assumed he was a fellow student—although she hadn't recognised him from her own political history course—albeit rather older than her. And, whilst she had laughed and flushed as she'd apologised, her embarrassment had been caused not by the fact that she had nearly run him down, and certainly not by the fact that she was doing something prohibited, but by the way he had made her feel, by the way her body and her emotions were already reacting to him, by the sudden rush of sensation flooding her mind and her body.

She had later admitted to him that if he had taken her there and then, in the middle of the quadrangle on the short, sweet grass, she doubted that she would have made any move to stop him. That was the kind of effect he had had on her, even though at the time she had still been a virgin and her experience of the opposite sex had been limited to Lloyd's chastely explorative kisses and attempts at a bit of mild petting.

When she had discovered that Sam was not, as she

had assumed, a fellow student, but a newly appointed junior classics lecturer, who had just completed his doctorate at Harvard, she had been completely mortified and shocked.

He had read her a mild lecture about riding her bicycle through a prohibited area and then sent her on her way, and she had not expected to see him again.

Only two days later he had turned up at her lodgings, carrying a book which had fallen out of the basket of her bike. She could remember how embarrassed she had been about the fact that he had discovered her almost in tears over a newspaper story she had been reading.

The article had been accompanied by heart-and conscience-rending photographs of grave-eyed starving children in the Third World, which had made Abbie exclaim passionately to Sam, once he had discovered the reason for her tears, that she could never bring a child into a world where so many, many children were so desperately in need.

'I expect you think I'm being over-emotional, don't you?' she had asked him self-consciously when she had herself back under control, but he had shaken his head.

'No, I don't,' he'd told her sombrely. 'As a matter of fact…'

He had never finished what he had been about to say because one of Abbie's fellow lodgers had returned, bounding into her room to request Abbie's assistance in the search for a borrowed book she had misplaced.

Sam had refused her offer of a cup of coffee, but it had been close to the beginning of the summer recess at the time, and to her astonishment, two weeks later, when she was lying in the garden of her parents' home sunbathing, he had turned up and invited her out.

He had explained later that he hadn't felt he was in a position to ask her out before, bearing in mind the fact that she was a student and he a lecturer. When he had explained that he'd felt uncomfortable about being thought of as the kind of lecturer who took advantage of his position to coerce young female students into sexual relationships with him, she had fallen even more deeply in love with him. He was so straightforward, so honest, so moral... Too moral on occasions...like the time he had refused to take her back to his rooms with him and make love to her.

'You don't want me,' she'd accused him tearfully.

In reply he had taken hold of her hand and placed it on his body. The strength and size of his erection beneath her hand had both shocked and excited her, and when he had seen the way her face flushed and she couldn't quite meet his eyes he had laughed and then sighed, gently lifting her hand away as he'd told her softly, 'You see, it's too soon and you're—'

'Don't you dare tell me I'm too young,' she had interrupted him passionately. 'I'm twenty...almost...'

'And I'm twenty-six...almost,' he had told her.

'That's only a difference of six years,' she had protested.

'You're a virgin still, and I'm not,' he had told her implacably. 'You're still playing in the shallows, whereas I—'

'I can learn. You can teach me...' she had told him fiercely. 'You...'

He had closed his eyes then and taken her in his arms.

'Oh, God, don't tempt me like that,' he had whispered to her, and his voice had been shaking—not with laughter, as she had first suspected, but with a mixture of emotions so potentially awesome and mind-blowing that she had trembled with excitement merely to think about them.

She had trembled as well when he had kissed her

properly the first time, and for many, many times after that.

But it hadn't just been sex…desire between them…

Abbie closed her eyes as the still painful memories engulfed her.

The first time Sam had kissed her properly had been on their second date. She had happened to mention that she wanted to go and see *A Midsummer Night's Dream*, which was being performed traditionally at Stratford, not intending to hint and certainly not expecting him to offer to take her there. The play had simply been extremely well reviewed and she had semi-hoped that her parents might offer to take her as a special treat.

When Sam had rung and said that he had got two tickets, and asked if she would like to go with him, she had been too breathless with excitement at the thought of seeing him again to co-ordinate her thoughts and ask any kind of logical or practical questions. So when he had arrived to collect her, fortunately a little early, dressed in all the formal elegance of a dinner suit, her mouth had parted in a soft 'oh' of surprised shock whilst her eyes had registered her shy but very whole-hearted and feminine approval of his sensually male elegance.

'I thought we could go somewhere and have some supper after the play,' he had suggested, as much to her parents as to her, Abbie had recognised, watching as her mother beamed her approval and her father coughed and muttered something about being sure he could trust Sam to get her home at a decent time.

Fortunately, long, floaty cotton dresses had been 'in' that year, and worn for everything from casual pub drinks to far more formal affairs. Hers had been new, the soft mixture of greens setting off her fair skin and blonde hair and matching her eyes quite spectacularly—or so the sales girl in the shop had told her. It had had a little high round neck, with cut-away sleeves and a keyhole cut out at the back, the soft cotton falling into a floaty A-line skirt.

The pretty white silk wrap her mother had rushed up-stairs to lend her had given the dress a more formal and elegant air, and Abbie remembered how she had blushed to the tips of her ears and curled her toes in her shoes as she'd felt her body's dangerous reaction to the way Sam had glanced oh, so briefly at her body, in such a way that it made her feel sure that he knew just how, beneath the thin cotton of her dress, her breasts were bare, her nipples tightening and pushing wantonly against the fine fabric...

It was over an hour's drive to Stratford, and for the first half of the journey Abbie had sat in blissful silence, too excited and overwhelmed by Sam's presence to make any attempt at conversation.

Later, she had managed to relax enough to comment that it had been a lovely day, and Sam had replied, equally gravely, that, yes, it had and that the rest of the week promised to be equally fine. Had she been sun-bathing? he had asked her casually.

'Yes,' she had agreed, adding that she had to be rather careful about going out in the sun because her skin was very fair and sensitive. She would never, she had ad-mitted ruefully, have the wonderful golden tan that other girls seemed to get so easily and which was so fashion-able.

They had been on a quiet stretch of road at the time, and Sam had turned his head and looked gravely at her before reducing the car's speed and reaching out to gently run his fingertips the full length of her bare arm. It was a gesture that had had her trembling with pleasure even before he had encircled her wrist and lifted it to his lips to caress the sensitive area where her pulse thudded visibly just beneath the surface.

'Your skin, like you, is perfect as it is,' he had told her huskily, and as his gaze had once again moved briefly to her breasts she had had a shockingly vivid mental image of his dark head bent over their nakedness whilst his mouth suckled first one sensitive tip and then the other.

Hurriedly she had looked away from him, half afraid that if he looked into her eyes he might actually read her thoughts.

The intensity of her own desire for him was still something she had not wholly come to terms with. By mutual consent she and Lloyd had agreed that, whilst they wanted to remain friends, friends was all they wanted to be; they still went out together occasionally, and they still enjoyed one another's company, but she had needed no proof that she had made the right decision in admitting to herself that, much as she liked Lloyd as a person, for them to have become lovers would have trapped them both in a relationship which could never go anywhere. She had found that out in the way she felt about Sam. Nothing had prepared her for physically reacting so intensely to a man, or her own growing emotional dependence on him.

She was already half afraid that she was in danger of falling in love with him. What else could explain her immediate and overwhelming attraction to him?

It had been a perfect summer's evening, the air sweet and balmy, the feel of Sam's dinner-suited arm against her bare skin as he helped her with her wrap and they walked away from the car towards the theatre deliciously exciting and sensual.

Very much aware of the interested and appreciative looks Sam was attracting from the female halves of other couples heading in the direction of the theatre, Abbie had felt proud and elated that he had chosen her as his date, as well as just a little bit wary that some other woman might try to take him away from her. He was, after all, a very compellingly attractive and male man: tall, broad-shouldered, with just a hint of muscle beneath his well-tailored suit, his dark hair thick and shiny, his eyes a bright, laughing blue and not cold at all, but rich and warm and full of silent messages she was half afraid to interpret.

The discovery that he had booked a private box for them had made Abbie stare at him in stunned delight.

'I've ordered us some champagne,' Sam whispered to her as they were shown to their seats. 'I hope you like it...'

'I love it,' Abbie fibbed, not wanting to admit that the only time she had really tasted it was at weddings, and then only the odd half-glass.

Her parents had been rather uneasy at first when, shortly after her eighteenth birthday, she had got herself a job working in a local hotel serving at the tables in the restaurant, but Abbie had insisted that she wanted the independence of feeling she was contributing towards her own upkeep, even though she knew they were more than willing, as well as able, to support her through university.

Once she had left home for university she had not told them at first that she had got herself a part-time job working in a small local pub, sensing that they would be concerned.

They knew now, though, but knew also that Abbie still avoided drinking alcohol herself. It was too expensive for one thing, and for another she didn't seem to have much of a head for it. But she would rather have died than confess to Sam that the champagne with which he had filled her glass just before the curtain went up tasted far too dry to her uneducated palate, and was already making her head swim slightly.

During the interval he took hold of her hand and asked her if she was enjoying herself and then added semi-harshly, 'I shouldn't be doing this. You do realise that, don't you?'

She wasn't really sure what he meant until he explained.

'You weren't meant to arrive in my life like this, not now... It's too soon and I'm not prepared, although how the hell can anyone ever be prepared for...? You're such a baby still,' he groaned as he removed the champagne glass from her trembling hand and took her in his arms. 'And the last thing I need is the kind of havoc that falling in love with you is going to cause in my life.

'I had everything so carefully planned,' he whispered against her lips as he caressed them gently with his own mouth, teasing them with light, delicate butterfly kisses which for some reason caused a dark flush to run up under his own skin, and his grip on her wrists as he held her away from his body tightened so much that it almost hurt.

'I'm sorry. I'm sorry,' he whispered remorsefully to her as he raised each wrist to his mouth in turn and kissed it gently. 'It's all your fault that I'm feeling like this...behaving like this,' he told her rawly. 'I've always thought of myself as sensible and level-headed, too cautious and logical to get involved in... You've made me realise that I hardly knew myself at all.'

'You can't be in love with me,' she had protested shakily, but her eyes had given away her real feelings and she had seen the way his own reflected that knowledge.

'No, I can't, can I...?' he drawled self-derogatorily.

'After all, I hardly know you…you hardly know me, and we haven't even been to bed together yet… How can I possibly be in love…?'

As she looked at him, her inhibitions relaxed by the cocktail of the champagne she had drunk and her own emotions, she told him bravely, 'I…I haven't been to bed with anyone. But…but I know I want to go to bed with you, Sam… I want it to be you who… I want it to be you,' she had finished in a soft, quavery little voice, and that was when he had kissed her properly for the first time in the darkened shadows of their box. Kissed her with his arms wrapped tightly around her, his body pressed against hers as his hands caressed her, his mouth hard and hot on hers, his tongue stroking her lips, coaxing them apart whilst she shivered with emotion and arousal, willing to give him anything, everything, if only he never took his mouth away from hers again.

She couldn't remember sitting through the rest of the play, but they must have done, and she couldn't remember much about the meal they'd had afterwards either. All she could remember was how much she had wanted to be alone with Sam, how much she had ached and yearned for him; how she had felt as he'd gently coaxed her to eat some of the dessert she had ordered and then felt unable to eat, lifting the spoon to her mouth, watching her whilst her lips parted and her face flooded with colour as her body and her senses recognised the sensuality, the sexuality of what he was doing, even whilst mentally she was still a stranger to such intense intimacy.

He had taken her straight home that evening, and on the evenings that had followed, but then, one Thursday, he had asked her how she and her parents would feel if he asked her to go away with him for a weekend…

'When?' had been her single, breathless response.

'I'll pick you up tomorrow morning,' he had told her.

Downstairs the telephone rang, but although she heard it she was still lost in the past. Abbie made no attempt to go and answer it. She didn't want to remember all this, she told herself frantically. She didn't want to relive it all again…to experience the pain of it all again. Not even from the safe distance of the years and the knowledge that separated her from it. But it was too late to hold back the memories, too late to stem the rushing tide sweeping down over her.

Please, no, she protested silently, but she knew it was no use. She had already allowed herself to remember too much, and she would now have to endure what she herself had set in motion. Her body trembling, she closed her eyes and gave in.

CHAPTER TWO

'I JUST can't believe this wonderful weather that we're having, and the forecasters are predicting that the heatwave is going to last at least another week...'

As Sam turned his head to look at her Abbie realised, with indignation, that he was laughing at her. He had picked her up from her parents' house half an hour ago, as arranged, firmly refusing to tell her where they were going as he placed her case in the boot of his car.

It had given her a funny little feeling inside to see her case nestling next to his, her heart giving a fierce, excited skip.

'What are you so nervous about?' Sam was asking her now.

'I'm not nervous,' Abbie denied untruthfully.

'Oh, yes, you are,' he told her softly. 'You always talk about the weather when you're nervous...'

'No, I do not,' Abbie protested, and then she looked at him and her heart melted, along with her nerves and her last-minute doubts about what she was doing.

'Don't be frightened,' Sam told her gently, the laughter disappearing from his eyes to be replaced by an emotion that made her head pound dizzily. 'No one's going to make you do anything you don't want to do...'

'But I do want to,' Abbie told him, and then blushed hotly and tried valiantly to hold his eyes as he looked straight into hers, praying that he wouldn't further tease her by demanding, You want to what? He didn't, but the look he was giving her was far more toe-curlingly explicit than any words could ever have been.

She still couldn't quite believe that he wanted her so much...that he was, as he'd told her himself, falling dangerously and completely in love with her.

Once during the journey, when she turned to look at him, her eyes widening as she saw the way his hands tightened slightly on the steering wheel, he told her huskily, begged, 'Please don't keep on looking at me like that. If you do I'm going to have to stop the car and take you in my arms and kiss the hell out of you, and once I start to do that...'

Abbie could feel her whole body, her face, starting to burn with the heat of what she was feeling. She could sense, see how dangerously close to losing control he was, and along with her instinctive sense of awe and virginal fear she also experienced a sharp thrill of feminine power and pleasure in the knowledge that she could have such an effect on him.

'The first time we make love I want it to be perfect for you, on a bed heaped high with the softest down and feather pillows, in a room that smells of roses and summer. I want to watch the sunlight on your body, high up in a turret, somewhere where we can be completely alone, just us and the sounds of nature and the living, breathing universe around us reaching us through narrow-latticed paned windows.

'Way, way below us there'll be a river, wide and slow-moving, the water soft and clear, and in the pool that it forms we'll swim together under a moonlit sky, and then we'll make love again on the grassy bank, still warm from the day's sunshine.

'The moonlight will turn your body to lissom silver. I'll follow its path with my hands and my lips. Your body will welcome mine with a sweet mixture of semi-pagan innocence and knowing that is in all women, a gift, but most especially in yours. Your skin will feel as cool as silk and only the hunting owl and the night sky will hear us when we cry out the unbearable ecstasy of our mutual need.'

'Stop it...stop it...' Abbie whispered shakily. Her whole body was on fire with arousal and desire for him, and she had a mad urgent impulse to beg him to stop the car and make love to her there and then.

There was a tight, aching need deep within her body, a pulsing that brought a hot flush of colour to her skin. How much further was the hotel he was taking her to? How much longer before...?

'Are you hungry? Would you like to stop somewhere for a drink and something to eat?' Sam asked her ten minutes later.

The prosaic question after the sensual seduction of his earlier words caught Abbie off guard. She shook her head, not trusting herself to speak. Surely he knew, must know, that the only sustenance she needed was him; the only appetite she had was for him.

Such wild and wanton thoughts were still unfamiliar enough to her to make her catch her breath and shyly avoid looking directly at him.

The road they were on had started to climb now; the countryside around them was changing. They were, Abbie recognised, driving through the Welsh borders, a wild, almost pagan part of the countryside she had secretly always thought incredibly romantic.

Here in this land once called the Welsh Marches, which still bore the visible scars of its medieval history in its ancient castles, it wasn't hard to mentally picture the armoured knights who had once patrolled these borders, to imagine one could still hear the faint clash of steel upon steel, the mingled cries of the injured and the victorious, to imagine as one drove past the derelict and sightless arrow slits of the castles that one had almost caught a glimpse of a pale, feminine wimpoled face watching anxiously from above.

'This is one of those places where the past feels very, very close, isn't it?' Sam's quiet comment, so closely echoing her own thoughts, made her shiveringly aware of how easily he could attune himself to her, of how much they seemed to share above and beyond the urgency of their sexual desire for one another.

She was still too young to fall in love helplessly and for ever, to commit herself to one man, one relationship for life and beyond, but she suspected that that was exactly what was going to happen to her.

It was not too late for her to change her mind, to call a halt to what was happening, she comforted herself; there was still time.

'Almost there now,' Sam told her.

The hotel was a fairy tale thing set in an almost magically perfect wooded valley, a cream stone, early Edwardian folly mansion designed as perfectly and as irresistibly as a Walt Disney castle straight out of *Sleeping Beauty*. A breathtaking jewel of a building, with its pale cream turrets and lichen-green tiled and scalloped roofs, set against a stunning backdrop of gently sloping protective hillsides clothed in softer green trees, surrounded by immaculately cared for lawns and flowerbeds dropping away to the river which ran through the bottom of the valley.

They had had to drive across a bridge over it to get to the main gates of the hotel and then up a sweeping cream stone drive. The hotel itself was hidden from view until the very last minute, Abbie's only sightings of it the tantalising glimpses she had caught of it as the road into the valley had spiralled down from the surrounding hills.

'It... It's...' She looked at Sam as he brought the car to a halt in the discreetly concealed car park to the rear of the hotel, which had obviously at some stage been a private home.

As she glanced towards the delicate turrets Abbie remembered how he had described making love to her. Then she had thought he was simply using his imagination. Now...

'I heard about it from one of the senior lecturers,' she heard him telling her quietly, answering her still unspoken question. 'He brought his wife here to celebrate their silver wedding anniversary.

'It was originally built by a very wealthy heiress as a secret hideaway where she could meet her lover. She came from a titled family connected to royalty and was destined for an arranged marriage. Her lover came from a different social circle. They would never have been allowed to marry, but every summer, from the year she married to the year he died, she came here to spend time with him.

'When he died she shut the house up, unable to endure it without him; she left it as a gift to his family.'

'How awful,' Abbie protested. 'To love someone like that all of your life and yet never be able to be truly together, to share. But always to have to keep your love a secret...' She shivered suddenly.

'What is it? What's wrong?' Sam asked her in concern.

'Nothing,' she fibbed. How could she tell him that the story he had told her had cast a cold little shadow over her own happiness, that she felt that somehow the place, beautiful though it was, was haunted by the unhappiness of a woman forced to hide her love and publicly deny it? It was as though somehow her unhappiness threatened to taint Abbie's own joy…as though her blossoming love would be spoilt and endangered.

Her thoughts were ridiculous, she told herself fiercely, especially when Sam had gone to so much trouble to make this, their first time together, as special and memorable as possible.

'Would I be correct in guessing that you've booked us a tower room?' she quizzed him, striving to throw off her sense of sadness and unease by smiling brightly at him.

'Now, why, I wonder, should you think that?' he teased her back as he removed their luggage from the boot of the car and then locked it.

It wasn't just a room he had booked for them, Abbie discovered ten minutes later, it was an entire suite with, she noticed, wide-eyed, not one but two bedrooms.

When she looked questioningly at him after the porter had left them, he explained quietly, 'I didn't want you to feel pressured in any way.'

'I don't,' Abbie told him equally gravely, her earlier mood forgotten now as her excitement at being with him filled her and her body started to react familiarly to his proximity to her.

'I *want* us to be lovers, Sam,' she told him shakily. 'I want it more than…I want *you* more than I ever imagined I could want any man. I want you so much that it hurts…here,' she told him breathlessly, hesitantly touching her body just above the small swell of her pubic bone. 'Here, where—'

She gave a small, half-protesting gasp as the rest of what she had been about to say was smothered by the fierce pressure of Sam's kiss.

Abbie felt herself start to tremble and then shudder in shocked delight as her body responded to his passion. She clung to his shoulders, her eyes glazed and her face flushed with the intensity of her own equally strong desire.

Sam lifted his mouth from hers to look down into her eyes, his hand cupping her face, his touch blissfully cool against her hot skin. Her senses were preternaturally attuned to him, and she could almost hear the rapid thud of his heart as well as see the swift rise and fall of his chest. She could feel the heat coming off his body, although, unlike hers, it was not so obviously nor hectically flushed, just a tell-tale burn of colour along his cheekbones coupled with the warm, musky smell of his arousal.

Did her own skin, her own body, smell equally sexually stimulating to him? she wondered dizzily. Did he breathe in the scent her desire had created and ache to press his lips, his open mouth, to her throat, her breast, her belly…her thighs?

A small sound, half protest, half ecstasy, caught in her throat, causing Sam to stroke her face tenderly and shush her, saying softly, 'It's all right. It's all right. I promise there's nothing for you to fear. I'll try not to go too fast…too—'

'I'm not afraid,' Abbie interrupted him, her body shaking as much as her voice. 'At least not of you…' Her eyes darkened, her mouth trembling slightly as she went on huskily, 'I'm afraid of what I feel, Sam, of how I feel. How much…how intensely. I'm afraid of being out of my own control and losing myself in what I feel…of wanting you so much…'

'I know, I know,' Sam groaned, wrapping her in his arms, her head against his chest as he rocked her gently. 'I feel the same way, and more. I'm afraid of not being able to give you the pleasure I want to give you, of not being able to hold back, of becoming so aroused that I *can't* hold back…'

'Do you wish that I wasn't a virgin?' Abbie asked him shakily. She felt him move as he cupped her face again and looked down at her.

'What on earth makes you think that?' he demanded huskily. 'Do you know how much I *love* the fact that you've chosen me to be your first lover? Even though I'm half terrified of disappointing you. Selfishly, I *like* knowing that you're not comparing me to someone else, wishing perhaps that I was someone else.'

He checked the protest she was about to make and told her warningly, 'I'm a man, Abbie, with all that that implies—possessive, even jealous sometimes, wanting *my* woman to be mine exclusively. I know—I *know* that once you *are* mine I will never, *ever* want another man to touch you...love you. Once you are mine...

'I'm twenty-six years old, and not inexperienced sexually, but when it comes to love...when it comes to love I'm as virginal as you, my sweet. Does that put *you* off me?'

Abbie's shining eyes gave him his answer.

'God, don't look at me like that,' he groaned. 'Not now. Not yet... I'd planned a walk through the gardens—the hotel is famous for them—afternoon tea on the lawn, a lazy, relaxing evening together, dinner with champagne, and—'

Abbie tugged impatiently on his sleeve and lifted her mouth to his.

'Kiss me, Sam,' she begged him huskily. 'Please, please, please kiss me.'

Ten minutes later, lying on the bed, her clothes—their clothes—strewn haphazardly all around them, Abbie watched anxiously as Sam studied her naked body. This was the first time he had seen her without all her clothes, and she had to fight an instinctive urge to wrap her arms around her breasts and roll over onto her stomach.

He was naked too, even if he had had to abandon his whispered instructions to her to remove his clothes and finish the task himself.

His body thrilled and excited her, and awed her slightly as well, reminding her that at twenty-six Sam wasn't a boy but a man.

She had seen Lloyd in his swimming trunks on countless numbers of occasions over the years, had seen his body develop from that of a gangling boy into that of a well-muscled nineteen-year-old, but he didn't look like Sam. No way did he look like Sam, whose shoulders were broad and whose stomach was flatter, whose body hair was...

Abbie could feel the heat rising through her body as she acknowledged what that soft covering of dark hair was doing to her insides. She wanted to reach out and touch it with her fingertips, to stroke it, to bury her face in it and breathe in its scent, to lick and kiss the skin it covered and, if she could actually be daring enough, to let her hand and her lips wander down along that straight dark path to its final destination. She wondered if Sam would be pleased or shocked by her wantonness, her desire to touch and taste the pure male essence of him.

But right now it was Sam who was looking at her, studying her, touching her, she realised, and a pulse jumped frantically in her throat as his fingertips pushed the long straight swathe of her hair out of the way and then traced the delicate shape of her collarbone.

To her chagrin she could see as well as feel that her nipples were already peaking, aching, her breasts, normally quite small and soft, suddenly much, much harder and fuller.

Did Sam like them? she wondered. Did he think they were too small, her nipples too little-girlie, all pink and tender, still those of a virginal girl rather than a woman?

He was not without sexual experience, he had said, and…

She tensed a little as Sam's hand cupped her breast, her head lifting so that she could look uncertainly into his eyes.

'They feel perfect,' he told her, his voice thick and slurred like melted honey, answering the question she had not yet asked.

'They *are* perfect,' he added even more throatily as he bent his head and gently kissed the hot, tight nipple sheltered by his hand, and then kissed it again, much less gently, much, much less gently, but oh, oh, so pleasurably, Abbie acknowledged as he slowly drew the taut point into his mouth and then sucked on it slowly, rubbing it with his tongue, making her feel…making her want.

Whimpering softly, she pressed closer to him, wanting him to repeat the caress, wanting to feel again that hot surge of pleasure his suckling had given her, which had arched right from the centre of her breast to her stomach, her womb, her thighs and that special, secret place she had tentatively explored in the early years of her sexual awakening, intrigued by and yet fearful of her dimly sensed awareness of its capacity for pleasure.

Instinctively she reached out to hold Sam's head against her breast, gasping in fresh excitement as she felt him stroking her stomach, his touch nerve-wrenching— tantalising, causing her to hold her breath and wonder if she dared reach out and urge his hand a little lower, or if— And then he moved slightly, one arm beneath her to lift her, the other brushing accidentally against the soft baby-fine blonde hairs that covered her sex.

Immediately she tensed, her body made rigid by the hot shaft of pleasure that jolted through her. She felt Sam freeze and knew that he was looking at her. When she raised her eyes to look at him she saw him shudder, his whole body heaving as he took a deep breath and demanded thickly, 'Already... You want me already?'

She didn't have to answer. His hand, his fingertips deft and yet oh, so tormentingly gentle were touching her, opening the outer lips of her sex, stroking her, feeling the warm wetness of her body's welcome and the eager way she pressed herself against his hand, mutely imploring him to touch her more intimately, to ease the ache that he himself had aroused within her with the rhythmic caress her body so urgently desired.

When he didn't she could actually feel herself starting to grind her teeth. His hand still covered her sex protectively but that wasn't what she wanted. What she wanted was...

She gave a small protesting moan of denial when he released her, reaching behind her for one of the pillows, easing it under her hips.

'This will make it easier, better,' he told her softly. His hands were shaking, she noticed, and the most sensitive part of his body was now stiffly erect. The sight of it made her want to reach out and run her fingers lovingly over its taut-skinned surface. The sight of it, of *him*, gave her a delicious, dangerous thrill of pleasure.

'Bend your knees,' Sam instructed her, showing her what he meant as he knelt between her open thighs, knelt between them and then, before she realised what he intended to do, bent his head and gently rubbed his face against her soft down.

The sensation of his tongue moving caressingly over her caused a scream to rise involuntarily in her throat. Automatically, Abbie tried to clamp down on it, but in the end she had to give voice to her sexual arousal and pleasure as Sam continued delicately to love the most intimate heart of her body, moving closer and closer to the tiny nub of flesh which was already pulsing and aching so tormentingly. She needed to feel him deep inside her, moving within her, slowly at first and then...

'Sam—Sam,' she protested chokily. 'I can't... I don't... Please...now... I...I want you. I want you inside me...very deep inside me. Now, now...*now*. I want you there now...always and for ever. I want—'

Abbie gasped as the rhythmic chant of her desire was suddenly cut off by the pressure of Sam's mouth against her own, his tongue flicking in and out of her lips as his hands held her, guided her, gentled the frantic movements of her body as she arched her back to meet and welcome the carefully protective invasion of his body.

It was just as she had wanted it to be, slow and sweet. A long, languorous pleasure, with her body drunk and dazed with sensual delight, her senses awash, flooded with the feel and heat of him so that even the tightness of his fit within her was somehow an extra small physical pleasure as she urged him deeper and deeper within her, finding from somewhere the knowledge to wrap herself around him and hold him, to move with him.

She climaxed before him, crying out in shocked pleasure and then later crying in earnest in his arms as the full emotional impact of what had happened overwhelmed her.

They spent almost the entire weekend making love, both in their room and, as he had whispered to her in the car on the way there, in the moonlight on a grassy bank beside the river.

By the end of the weekend they both knew there was no going back, that their love for one another was more powerful than anything they had ever experienced before. Too powerful for them to ignore or control.

'I didn't want it to be like this,' Sam told her. 'You're so young...too young...'

'We could just be lovers, and—' Abbie began, but he interrupted her immediately.

'No...' he said harshly, and then, more softly, 'That isn't what I want; you know that, Abbie. This isn't just about sex. It's about... It's about finding the woman I want to spend the rest of my life with. It's about loving you so intensely that I want to keep you here with me and never let you out of my sight. Falling in love with each other like this might not be what we planned, but...'

'Take me back to bed,' she whispered coaxingly, her voice shivering with desire. 'We've still got time before we have to leave...'

They were married three months later, in spite of her parents' pleas to her to wait and Lloyd's dogmatic assertion that she was a fool to tie herself down so young.

Lloyd and Sam did not like one another. Lloyd felt that Sam was rushing her into marriage and Sam, rather to Abbie's secret feminine delight and amusement, was intensely jealous of Lloyd, seemed unable to believe that there had never been anything other than the mildest boy-and-girl affection between them.

'You say that now, but he loves you and you must have felt something for him, otherwise you wouldn't have gone out with him for so long.'

'We're friends, that's all,' Abbie told him lovingly. But she could see that he wasn't entirely convinced.

Four months after they had first met they were married, and two months after that Abbie discovered that she was pregnant.

A few months of happiness—a happiness so intense that she had foolishly believed that nothing could ever damage or destroy it. But she had been wrong, and the pain she had suffered because of that misjudgement had been far, far more intense than the pleasure that had gone before it.

It had left her scarred and damaged, unable to take the risk of ever trusting another man, and hating her ex-husband with a hatred that still burned just as strongly in her today as it had done on that day all those years ago, when he had stared at her across the kitchen of the pretty house he had bought them close to the university and told her harshly, 'You're pregnant? But you can't be. It's impossible.'

CHAPTER THREE

'IMPOSSIBLE...wh-what do you mean?' Abbie had stammered, her face white with shock and disbelief. She had been so thrilled when the doctor had confirmed what she had secretly already suspected to be true—that she had conceived Sam's child.

They hadn't talked about having a family as yet, but of course she had believed that ultimately they would have children.

If her timing was right, she would at least just about be able to get through her finals before the baby's birth. She had chuckled out loud as she'd left the doctor's surgery, her face bright with love and joy as she'd hugged the pleasure of her news to herself.

She couldn't wait to tell Sam. He would be a wonderful father. She could see him now, his large hands cradling their child.

She hoped it would be a boy...at least this first one. They could turn the small fourth bedroom into a nursery. All right, so maybe she wouldn't take up the career she had originally planned, but Sam earned more than enough to support both of them. All of them, she'd amended, and at least she would have her degree.

Whilst the baby—the babies—were young, she wanted to be at home with them, but later, even though by then she would be positively ancient, close on thirty, she could, if she wanted, embark on a career—just so long as it wasn't something that conflicted with her family life, her husband, their children. They would always come first.

She'd been so happy she could have burst. She'd
wanted to go to Sam right then and tell him their wonderful news, but he would have been right in the middle
of a lecture, and besides...she'd wanted to have him to
herself when...

Pregnant...a baby...Sam's baby. She was the luckiest,
luckiest girl in the whole wide world.

Suddenly she'd felt ravenously hungry. Sardines...
sardines on toast; that was what she wanted—yes, and
then an enormous sticky bar of chocolate fudge.

She would, of course, have to start eating very carefully. She had the baby to think of now, she'd warned
herself sternly, but for now...for today she could afford
to be a little self-indulgent...just as she probably had
been when this baby had been conceived. She'd given a
small chuckle. When the doctor had asked her if she had
any idea when conception had taken place she had fur-
rowed her forehead and frowned.

'When did you last have sex?' he had asked her pa-
tiently.

'This morning,' she had answered promptly, and had
then flushed a brilliant shade of pink as she'd realised
what he was getting at.

'Er...I'm not sure. It could have been... I missed my
first period three weeks ago...'

She had been taking the pill, but she had been so busy
that for two consecutive nights she had forgotten to take
it. This baby was obviously meant to be...just like the
way she and Sam had met—just like their love. Oh, God,
she'd been so happy...so very, very happy...

'I mean that it's impossible for you to be pregnant—
at least not with my child,' Sam told her now, harshly.

Abbie looked at him in mute disbelief. Where her face
had originally been flushed with excitement and happiness it was now bone-white. Sam's, on the other hand,

bore the tell-tale signs of male anger in the dark colour staining his cheekbones and the clenched tightness of his jaw.

'What do you mean, not with your child? Is this some kind of joke?' Abbie whispered in confusion.

She didn't know what Sam meant; she couldn't understand what he was saying. How could her baby, *their* baby, not be his? Of course it was his—theirs. What on earth was he trying to do to her? If this was his idea of some kind of teasing game…

Anxiously she searched his face, but there was no sign of any good humour or amusement in it. Just the opposite.

'A joke? My God, I wish it was,' Sam told her harshly. 'You cannot be carrying my child, Abbie, because I cannot give you a child. I've had a vasectomy.'

'You've what? You *can't* have done. Not without telling me. Not without…'

'I had it done several years ago, when I was in India with VSO. I was working in a small village; a young man I met there, a young man of my own age, the son of the head man, who had taken me under his wing, told me that he intended to have a vasectomy. I was shocked at first, wondering how on earth he could contemplate such a thing, but then he took me on a tour of Bombay and pointed out to me the number of children who had been abandoned because their parents could not afford to feed them. He told me the basic economics of what happened in a world when there were too many mouths to feed, when the land itself could not support them.

'"What is best?" he asked me. "That I prevent conception now or that I wait until my children are one, four…seven, and watch them die slowly of malnutrition?"

'What he said, what he showed me, shocked me, made

me realise that to father a child when there were already so many, many children in the world in need was an act of selfishness which would simply push those children even further down the poverty scale.

'I decided to have a vasectomy myself.'

Abbie stared at him.

'You're lying,' she told him flatly.

'No,' Sam denied. '*You* are the one who is doing that, Abbie, when you claim that you are carrying my child.'

Abbie licked her lips nervously. She couldn't believe this was happening. How could it be happening? How could she possibly be carrying Sam's child in her womb when he…? Tears filled her eyes, a mixture of anguish, anger and panic exploding inside her.

'You must have known I would want children, and yet you married me without telling me that you couldn't give me any. Why? Why…?'

'Would you believe me if I told you that I was so much in love with you…wanted you so desperately that the thought of children or anything else other than our love simply never occurred to me? And for your information I did *not* know you would want children. I thought you possibly shared my feelings about the world not being able to support the children it already has. It hasn't ever been something we've discussed.'

'Because there hasn't been any time…any need. But you must have known…must have realised…'

'Why?' Sam demanded more harshly. 'Because it's what everybody does…what everyone wants?'

'You lied to me…you deceived me,' Abbie wept.

The look he gave her was full of bitter contempt.

'And you haven't done the same to me? Tell me something, Abbie,' he demanded savagely. 'How long exactly was it after I had had you that you went crawling into his bed? A month, a week…less…?'

'What...what do you mean? I haven't...' Abbie protested hotly, her face flushing as she realised what he was saying.

How dared he accuse her of sleeping with someone else? How dared he accuse her of anything?

'Oh, come on; don't play the innocent. It's hardly an appropriate role for you now, is it? You might have fancied passing yourself off to me and the rest of the world as an innocent young madonna, but what you actually are is little better than a whore, passing off her bastard child on someone else—or, rather, trying to. Unfortunately for you it's just not going to work.

'It's his, I imagine? Dear, wonderful Lloyd? I saw him driving away the other evening just before I got home. Does he know you're carrying his child yet? Does he...?'

'I'm not carrying Lloyd's child,' Abbie denied, shocked. What was Sam trying to imply? She and Lloyd had never been lovers. The very thought of having a sexual relationship with him filled her with the same kind of horror she would have felt had he actually been her brother. She and Lloyd were close, yes, but not in any sexual way. Lloyd had simply called round to see her to talk to her about some problems he was having with his university course.

He had stayed longer than he had intended and had then had to dash off without waiting to say hello to Sam.

That Sam or anyone else should even remotely consider that she and Lloyd would have an affair and that, even worse, she would try to foist his child off on her husband was so totally and utterly ridiculous an idea that she instantly, once again, wondered if Sam was trying to play some kind of bizarre joke on her.

He did like to tease her occasionally, she knew, because—or so he said—he loved watching the pink colour flood her face when he did. But so far he had certainly shown no inclination to play the kind of elaborate and cruel practical joke on her which would give rise to his denial of their child. To do so would have been totally out of character for him, she was sure. But then she had not really known him so very long, had she? And, like her assumption that they would have children together, she had taken his gentleness and lack of any cruel or malicious streak on trust.

But surely she would have known, sensed, guessed if…

But she hadn't known that he had had a vasectomy, had she? And, if he hadn't thought it necessary to pass such a vital fact about himself on to her, what other vital information might he also be concealing?

'Y-you can't possibly believe that Lloyd and I are anything other than friends,' she stammered chokily. 'I've told you…'

'Why not? Someone has to be the father of this child you thought you'd pass off as mine…'

'But you're the only man I've ever slept with…the only man I've ever loved,' she could have added. But for some reason she held the words back. To talk of love in the present circumstances would be not just acutely painful but almost an act of sacrilege.

'I know how hot in bed you are—after all, I've had more than enough proof of it,' he added cruelly. 'But if I wasn't satisfying you you should have said—'

'Sam, please don't,' Abbie interrupted him, her voice breaking as she reached out to him, but he stepped back, an expression of such cold disdain in his eyes that she physically flinched away from it.

'I thought you were perfect, wonderful, a dream come to life. I told myself I was the luckiest man on earth...wondered what I'd ever done to be so lucky. But all the time all you were was a mirage...a sham...'

As she listened to him, suddenly Abbie felt as though she was looking at a stranger, a stranger who bore no resemblance to the man she had married, the man she had fallen in love with. That Sam had been warm and gentle, compassionate, loving. This Sam was cruel and cold, savagely uncaring of her feelings...uncaring of anything other than what he chose to believe. He accused her of lying to him, but he was the one who had deceived her, Abbie decided angrily.

How dared he speak about her in such sexually derogatory terms? And if she had been sexually eager, well, that had simply been because...because she had loved him so much.

Had loved him...?

As Abbie looked across the space that divided them a feeling of intense pain and anger filled her.

'I don't care what you say, Sam,' she told him quietly. 'I have never been unfaithful to you.'

'No, of course not,' he jeered. 'Of course the child you're carrying is mine...'

'No,' Abbie told him gently. 'No, Sam. He or she is not yours. The baby...*my* baby is exactly that—mine.'

As she turned on her heel and walked towards the door, he demanded, 'What are you doing? Where are you going?'

'I'm going upstairs to pack my things,' she told him with brave dignity, 'and then I'm leaving.'

'Abbie...'

'What?' she asked him. 'You're sorry? You take back everything you said? It's too late, Sam. You see, even if you told me now that you didn't really mean any of those horrible things you've just said, even if you swore that you loved me, that you wanted me and our...my child, I wouldn't believe you. I'd know you were lying, deceiving me—just as you deceived me by default about your vasectomy.

'It isn't just our child's right to your love and protection as its father that you've just destroyed, Sam, it's everything else as well. My trust...my faith...my love... But do you know what hurts me most of all?' she asked him, her eyes glittering with the tears she was too proud to allow to fall.

'What hurts me most isn't the cruel things you've said about me...the lies... What hurts me most is that you've never even stopped to ask yourself if you could be wrong...if you could have made a mistake...if there could be some way—'

'Because I know it's impossible,' he interrupted her fiercely. 'It just isn't possible for you to have conceived my child.'

'No? *That* isn't what my body says,' she told him steadily. 'But there's no need for you to worry about it, Sam. In fact I'd rather you didn't. From now on I'd rather you stayed right out of my life, as I intend to do yours. From now on, as far as I'm concerned, you simply don't exist. Rather appropriate, don't you think? When our child—my child—asks about his or her father I shall simply tell it that you don't exist.'

'Abbie...'

She could hear the note of pleading desperation beneath the anger in his voice, but she closed her ears to it.

It was over...finished... How could it be any other way?

She placed her hand on her stomach as she walked away from him and whispered softly, 'Don't worry, my precious one. I love you...I'll always love you.'

She wanted nothing more to do with Sam, she told

her family and friends. Nothing more to do with her marriage. Her baby and its safety, its future were all that concerned her now, she had told everyone, with a calm detachment which she knew had surprised and slightly disconcerted those who thought they knew her. Her previous easygoing, eager-to-please personality seemed to have changed overnight into one of cool, icy strength. The warmth and passion, the intensity which had been so much part of her emotional, loving nature was firmly banished as she took on the new role that nature—and Sam—had imposed on her.

When Sam tried to get in touch with her to 'talk things through' she refused to have anything to do with him.

She wanted nothing from him, she informed her parents. The house, the furniture, the wedding presents—she wanted none of them.

But how would she manage? they asked her in concern. On her own with a baby... She would, of course, have their help, their support, but...

'I'll find a way,' she told them determinedly.

Sam wanted to give her an allowance, but she refused that as well.

'I don't want his charity,' she told her solicitor. 'I don't want anything of his.'

'But you're carrying his child,' her solicitor had pointed out gently.

'No,' Abbie denied woodenly. 'This child is mine. Only mine.'

Nothing and no one could persuade her to change her mind. Her parents were shocked by the implacable streak of stubborn determination revealed in their hitherto gently malleable daughter.

Not to them, not to anyone could she confess that during that dreadful fight with Sam, when he had accused her of carrying another man's child, of being unfaithful to him and breaking not just her marriage vows but the vows of love she had made to him that first night she had spent in his arms, something inside her had been destroyed, had quite simply ceased functioning…had been broken. And it could never be repaired.

She never wanted it to be repaired because she never again wanted to go through the kind of pain that Sam had put her through. Ever…

It was hard at first, and her parents were horrified when she grimly insisted on carrying on working in a local pub right up until the last month of her pregnancy.

She was living at home with them then, having nowhere else to go. Sam had been threatened with an injunction if he ever tried to see her, and she had heard in a roundabout way that he intended to leave the country to take up a post he had applied for at an Australian university. She had been surprised by her own lack of reaction to that news. She had quite simply felt nothing.

Towards the end of her pregnancy a sense of great calm descended on her, a sense of purpose, a need to gear her whole life towards the arrival of her baby.

Although as yet she had said nothing to her parents, she intended just as soon as she could to find herself a small flat somewhere, which she could rent for her and the baby. She didn't want to be dependent on her parents for ever, loving and protective though they were. She had already talked to the landlady of the pub about returning to her job as soon as she could, and of working longer hours. She knew it wasn't going to be easy but she also knew that somehow she would find a way… She had to for her baby's sake.

She had to and she would.

*   *   *

'Mum, Mum, where are you?'

Abbie gave a small start as she realised just how long she must have been sitting on the dusty loft floor, lost in her memories of the past. Her body felt cold and cramped, her head filled with old memories. Quickly she stuffed her wedding dress back out of sight, wincing as her cramped muscles protested at the movement, calling out to Cathy, 'I'm on my way down, Cathy. Put the kettle on, would you, darling?'

CHAPTER FOUR

'WHERE on earth have you been? I rang twice and there was no reply so I decided to come round,' Abbie heard her daughter saying as she hurried into the kitchen.

'I was upstairs in the loft,' Abbie explained. 'That's why I didn't hear the phone.'

'The loft? What on earth…? Mum, are you all right?' Cathy asked anxiously, concern darkening her eyes as she turned round to look at her mother.

'Of course I'm all right,' Abbie told her. 'Why shouldn't I be?'

'No reason. It's just… Look, you're not upset because of what I said earlier, are you?' Cathy demanded in a rush. 'I didn't mean to upset you. I…I know you don't like talking about Dad…'

'Oh, Cathy, of course I'm not upset,' Abbie denied remorsefully, going over to put her arms around her daughter and hug her lovingly.

'I do know how hard it must be for you, darling, especially now, when you and Stuart are planning your wedding. I know it can't have been easy for you growing up without a father, knowing that yours…that he… If I was snappy because you mentioned him, I suppose it was just because you might have thought you saw someone who looked like him, but it can't possibly have been Sam. He would never come back here. He knows that there's no way I'd ever forgive him for what he did and he knows that he has no place in our lives. He gave up any rights he had to that when he denied that you were his child.'

52

'I know how much he hurt you, Mum,' she heard Cathy saying in a muffled voice. 'But it must have been a shock for him too, to learn that you were pregnant when he believed that that wasn't possible. Stuart says that any man would be shocked, and—'

'"Stuart says"?' Abbie queried, releasing her daughter and stepping back slightly to look up into her face. Her heart sank as she saw the way Cathy's gaze slid away from her own, her face slightly flushed, her expression unfamiliarly defensive.

'Mum, I don't want to hurt you, but—'

'Then let's forget the whole subject,' Abbie interrupted her gently. 'The fact that your father has no place in our lives is by his own choice, remember. Anyway, what exactly are you doing here?' she queried lightly. 'I thought you and Stuart were house-hunting this evening.'

Cathy had moved into Stuart's small bachelor flat several months ago, but both of them had agreed that they wanted to start their married lives in a home which they had chosen together. Stuart was in the fortunate position of having secured a good job with a local firm of accountants, and his parents had already announced that their wedding present to the young couple would be a lump sum towards their new home.

Abbie, although she had said nothing to her daughter, suspected that Stuart's family were slightly surprised by her own initial reaction to the engagement, which had been to counsel the young couple not to rush into anything. In their eyes, and in the eyes of most other people, Abbie acknowledged, Stuart was excellent husband material, with his steady family background and his secure financial future.

'Yes. Yes, we are,' Cathy agreed quietly. 'But I just

wanted to see you first. 'Mum—' Cathy started to say, but Abbie interrupted her, warning her.

'That sounds like Stuart's car now, Cathy, and I've really got to rush myself. I hadn't realised how long I'd been up in the loft and I've got a meeting with Dennis Parker in an hour...'

'What, at the hotel?' Cathy asked her anxiously.

'Mmm... Cathy, what is it?' Abbie asked, but her telephone had begun to ring and Stuart was already knocking on the back door.

'Give me a ring and tell me how the house-hunting went,' Abbie told her, kissing her lovingly before giving her a small push in the direction of the back door and then rushing into the hall to answer her telephone.

She was still smiling slightly ruefully to herself half an hour later as she stepped out of the shower and started to towel her body dry.

Cathy was such a loving, caring girl—everyone said so. It was typical of her that she should worry that she had upset her mother by bringing up the subject of her father.

She hoped that Stuart and his family appreciated what a lucky man he was, and that he took good care never to hurt Cathy the way Sam had hurt her.

Her smile turned to a frown as she remembered what Cathy had said when she'd repeated Stuart's comment about Sam. It was, Abbie reflected, perhaps only natural that Stuart should view what had happened from a male perspective...from Sam's point of view. But...

But what? But she hadn't liked hearing Cathy voice Stuart's comments? Her daughter had to grow up and away from her some time, she reminded herself. She couldn't stay a little girl for ever. She and Stuart were very deeply in love, and, like any girl in love, it was only natural that she should attach the preface 'Stuart says' to so many of her comments, for a little while at least. She, as Cathy's mother, must just learn to grit her teeth and try to hold onto her sense of humour—and to her memories of how she had felt when Cathy had first started school and begun every other sentence with the words 'Mrs Johnson says'.

This was the pitfall that lay in wait for every mother, Abbie told herself. Perhaps all the more so in cases like hers when, as a single parent with only one child, she knew the relationship between Cathy and herself had been so very close.

Had been?

Abbie sighed as she padded into her bedroom and opened a drawer to remove clean underwear.

Cathy had often teased her warningly about her habit of walking around naked before she'd left home for university; that was one of the benefits of living either alone or in a single-sex household, Abbie acknowledged as she pulled on clean white briefs, tugging them up over her still enviably slender hips. Her body wasn't something Abbie was used to spending much time thinking about; so long as it and she were both healthy and functioned properly she was content.

The thought of finding it necessary to be sexually alluring was one which had filled her with angry repugnance in the early years after Sam's desertion and betrayal, and she'd been filled with a bitter distrust of virtually all men. But, more recently, this had become something she viewed with detached amusement when she listened to those of her friends of the same age who were beginning to mourn the passing of their youth.

That was just one of the benefits that came from living a manless existence; the fact that she was now over forty wasn't something that Abbie felt in the least uncomfortable about.

When other people commented admiringly, as they frequently did, that she looked nowhere near her age, she generally told them gently that, on the contrary, she looked exactly her age, and that if they bothered to look around and use their eyes they would see that most women of forty looked exactly what they were; adult, fully grown human beings at the full height of their maturity and often with a hell of a lot more going for them than they had ever had as callow young things in their late teens and early twenties. And if the male sex failed to appreciate the fact then that was their problem.

Although, to be fair, she admitted judiciously as she wriggled into a stretch calf-length slim-fitting black skirt and then pulled a cream knitted top over her head, men were beginning to catch on to the fact that a woman in her forties was still very much a sexually alluring and active human being—rather too much, as far as she was concerned.

She had had more men approach her in the years since she had reached her fortieth birthday than in the previous decade, including several who she suspected were a good half-dozen years or more younger than she was herself.

Not that she had been interested in any of them.

She glanced at her wristwatch as she fastened it. She didn't want to be late for her meeting with Dennis. They had established a good working rapport in the time that he had been in charge of the town's most prestigious hotel, and both of them in their different ways were perfectionists when it came to their work. Abbie saw him strictly as a business associate, but, as Fran had pointed out teasingly to her on more than one occasion, Dennis would leap at any chance she gave him to put their relationship on a more personal footing.

'No way,' Abbie had told her firmly.

'You can't go on being afraid for ever, Abbie,' Fran had told her gently.

'I'm not afraid,' Abbie had denied. 'I just don't see the point in getting involved in a relationship I know I don't really want.'

'But surely there must be times when—' Fran had begun gently.

'When what?' Abbie had interrupted her. 'When I need a shoulder to cry on...? A man to lean on...? Sex...?' She had shaken her head vigorously. 'No. Never. Don't feel sorry for me, Fran,' she had warned her friend, correctly reading her expression. 'I certainly don't feel sorry for myself. The last thing I want is any kind of emotional complications in my life.'

'He must have hurt you so very badly—Cathy's father,' Fran had said sympathetically.

'No,' Abbie had told her curtly. 'I hurt myself by believing him when he said he loved me.'

As she inspected her face in her mirror, checking her make-up, Abbie decided wryly that, whilst other people might think she looked young, when she compared herself to Cathy she could certainly see the difference between them.

Her eyes grew slightly shadowed for a second. Cathy had mentioned Sam quite a lot over the last few months, asking her questions about him, bringing his name into their conversations... Stuart's influence, Abbie suspected.

Abbie had never made any secret of the facts of her marriage and its break-up, answering Cathy's questions as she'd asked them, tailoring her answers to meet the emotional awareness of her age at the time the questions had been asked.

Cathy knew what had happened, how Sam had turned his back on them both.

It disturbed her that Cathy should have imagined that she had seen him. That was impossible, of course, but what upset her was that the tone of Cathy's voice had implied that she might actually *want* to have seen him.

She had thought that she had succeeded in being both mother and father to Cathy until now, until she had seen that look in Cathy's eyes when she'd talked about her father—her *father*. Sam had *never* been a father to Cathy.

'Abbie…'

Abbie smiled, stepping back from Dennis slightly as he came forward to greet her, gently fending him off with her outstretched hand as she avoided the kiss he had obviously intended to give her.

'You said you wanted to see me about the extra staffing requirements over the Christmas and New Year period,' she reminded him gently.

'What…? Oh, yes… You know, Abbie,' he told her eagerly, 'you really are the most stunningly attractive woman I—'

'Not *the* most, surely,' Abbie teased him lightly, but her eyes held a warning message, reminding him that she wasn't here to be flirted with.

'Very well.' Dennis gave in. 'Let's get down to business, then. I thought we could talk over dinner, if that's all right with you. We've taken on a new chef and—'

'I know,' Abbie interrupted him. 'Trained by the best, according to my informants. Quite a coup…'

'An expensive one,' Dennis agreed. 'But the area isn't short of good restaurants, and the last thing we want is hotel guests eating elsewhere because we can't provide them with a first-class meal.'

'People often find that hotel restaurants lack the intimacy of somewhere smaller.'

'Mmm. I know,' Dennis agreed as he ushered her out

of the foyer and into the restaurant. 'But I'm hoping that by offering a special price for our Saturday evening dinner-dances we'll bring more people in, and that once they've tasted David's food they'll want to come back. You'll have to tell me what you think of it.'

'Don't worry, I shall,' Abbie laughed.

The restaurant was comfortably busy for a midweek evening, but then the hotel was busier during the week than at weekends, mainly with businessmen and women.

'How's the leisure centre doing?' Abbie asked as they sat down and the waiter brought them both a menu.

'Not too badly,' Dennis responded.

'You've got quite a lot of competition, and your prices are on the high side,' Abbie pointed out.

'Yes, but we also have a more up-market setting, plenty of free parking and a certain degree of exclusivity...'

'Mmm, there's such a thing as pricing yourself out of the market,' Abbie warned him as she gave the waiter her order.

'How many extra staff do you think you're going to need?' she asked him whilst they waited for their food. 'And remember,' she reminded him, 'since they'll be working over Christmas and New Year, and especially since most of them will be young and female, I can only supply them with your assurance that they'll be provided with guaranteed transport to and from work.'

'They'll have access to our normal free staff bus service,' Dennis told her.

Abbie shook her head.

'That's not good enough, Dennis. I don't want any of my girls having to walk to and from pick-up points which might mean them having to walk alone and in the dark, late at night. You'll have to do better than that. You know my feelings on that subject...'

'I certainly do,' Dennis groaned. 'Have you any idea of what it costs to run a door-to-door pick-up service for every single member of staff?'

'Have you any idea what it costs a young girl when she's sexually harassed or worse?' Abbie returned crisply, shaking her head as she told him firmly, 'No, Dennis, I'm insistent on this. There's no way I'd allow any of my staff to work late shifts without guaranteed transport home.'

'I can only do that by offering them a lower rate of pay,' Dennis warned her.

'Rubbish,' Abbie denounced, taking a mouthful of her starter. 'Mmm, this is good,' she told him, 'and I'm glad to see that your chef realises that eye-appeal on its own isn't enough. I must admit I've grown rather tired of a pretty plateful of artistically designed half-cold and semi-tasteless food, and I'm glad to see you're including a good choice of vegetarian dishes, and not just the obligatory omelette.'

'We're getting more and more demand for them, and one of this guy's specialities is his range of health-conscious dishes.

'Have *you* made any plans for Christmas this year?' Dennis asked.

Abbie shook her head.

'How are the plans for the wedding coming along?' Dennis questioned, after they had been served with their main courses.

'They're not,' Abbie admitted ruefully.

'Well, you know if you decide to hold the wedding breakfast here we'll give you a good deal,' he told her.

'Yes,' Abbie agreed.

Stuart's mother had already suggested to her that it might be a nice idea to hold the wedding reception in a marquee in their large garden, and Abbie had been forced to acknowledge privately that she was probably quite right. The only thing was that she rather suspected that given half the chance Stuart's mother—for entirely the best and most generous of reasons—might be rather inclined to take over the organisation of the whole wedding. Both of Stuart's sisters were already married, and Abbie had to admit that Stuart's mother had the expertise to organise a flawlessly perfect wedding. But Cathy was *her* daughter and she…

She what? she asked herself dryly. She felt jealous… pushed out…usurped.

By rights she knew she ought to be more than grateful to Stuart's parents for their offer to take over not only the wedding arrangements but the financial cost as well. There was certainly no way she could afford to pay for an occasion as glittering and expensive as they could put on, despite the success of her business—which was modest in contrast to the financial resources of Stuart's parents.

And she had seen the faint look of hesitation in Cathy's eyes when she had tentatively suggested holding the reception for her at the hotel.

'Wouldn't it be rather anonymous?' Cathy had asked uncertainly.

'Perhaps,' Abbie had agreed, her heart sinking a little. 'Still, you've got plenty of time to think about it, darling. After all, you haven't even set a proper date yet.'

'No, I know, but Stuart's mother says that all the very best places get booked up simply ages in advance, and that with Gina's wedding they had to change the date twice because they couldn't get the caterers they wanted, and then the florist only fitted them in because she had done Gina's cousin's wedding.

'She had her reception at this fabulous hotel,' Cathy had gone on wistfully. 'It's about half an hour's drive from here, and from the way Gina described it it sounds heavenly. It's a small, privately owned hotel that was once a house. It was built by this very rich aristocrat so that she could be with her lover…'

Abbie had felt her stomach start to churn with a mixture of shock and nausea as Cathy continued with her description.

She knew exactly where Cathy meant, of course, although she had not told her daughter that, saying curtly instead, 'It's far too far away, Cathy—over an hour's drive, and—'

'Only half an hour,' Cathy had corrected her. 'The new motorway extension runs within a few miles of it. But you're right, of course, it is out of the question. It's quite horrendously expensive.'

'Don't worry, darling,' Abbie had reassured her, regretting her own reaction. 'Your wedding will be equally special, I promise you.'

'I know that, Mum,' Cathy had agreed, hugging her. 'After all, it's the man you're marrying that's important, the way you feel about one another. It's just…' She'd wrinkled her nose slightly. 'Well, I can't help feeling sometimes that Stuart's mother feels that Stuart could have done better. She never says anything, but…'

'Rubbish. Stuart is a very, very fortunate young man,' Abbie had informed her firmly.

'You're only saying that because you're my mother,' Cathy had laughed.

'And Stuart's mother is only saying what she says because she's *his* mother,' Abbie had pointed out. 'All mothers want the best—the very, very best—for their children, and that's only natural,' Abbie had told her. 'But never forget that you *are* the best, Cathy. Never let anyone make you feel otherwise, and if Stuart doesn't believe that, if he doesn't believe that you are better than the best, then he isn't worthy of you.'

'Oh, Mum,' had been Cathy's slightly tearful response.

'You know that comment I made earlier about you,' Dennis murmured to her, breaking into her thoughts as he leaned across the table towards her. 'Well, don't look now, but there's a man seated at a table to your left who obviously thinks exactly the same thing. He hasn't taken his eyes off you all evening.'

'I think that's rather an exaggeration,' Abbie told Dennis dryly, and she obeyed his admonition to turn her head and look slightly to her left feeling only mild curiosity.

The man seated at the table Dennis had indicated looked right back at her, his expression neither mild nor curious.

Abbie felt the room start to spin dangerously around her, her body ice-cold with shock as she found herself looking straight into the instantly recognisable eyes of her ex-husband: the man who, she had so recently sworn to her daughter, *their* daughter, would never come back.

The man who had stolen her love, broken her heart and come close to destroying her whole life.

Abbie stared at him, her face, her body, her thoughts turned to stone, unable to function on even the most basic level, unable to look away, to move, to do anything. From a distance she heard a vaguely familiar buzzing sound, and then Dennis was standing up, cursing faintly under his breath as he apologised.

'I'm sorry, Abbie, someone's buzzing me. I'd better go and find out what's wrong. I'll be as quick as I can. If you want the sweet trolley…'

Although Abbie heard him she was completely unable to make any kind of response. Shock had picked her up on a giant icy wave, flinging her down in a place that was totally unfamiliar and alien. She knew her surroundings and yet she didn't know them, didn't know how they had come to be invaded, taken over, possessed by this man who should have been on the other side of the world.

'No…'

As she heard the feeble denial whisper past her numb lips Abbie saw Sam get slowly to his feet and, still holding her gaze, start to walk towards her.

She wanted to get up, to run away, to escape before it was too late, but for some reason she just couldn't move.

'Abbie…' His voice sounded gravelly and heart-sickeningly familiar. She could feel herself starting to tremble from head to foot, as though every single physical part of her was responding to the husky resonance of his voice. But where once she had trembled with passion and love, now she trembled with shock and fury.

How dared he do this to her? How dared he be here? How dared he simply appear in the middle of her world…her life? And most of all how dared he simply walk towards her as though…as though…?

'Abbie…'

He had hardly changed at all, she recognised. If anything, he looked even better, even more devastatingly and sensually male than he had done before. His hair was still as thick, and almost as dark as ever, the small touches of silver just beginning to show in its darkness more an added attraction rather than a detraction from his magnetic good looks.

His skin looked tanned, his body beneath its sophisticated and expensive suiting moved just as easily, just as malely as she remembered, and his eyes were just as brilliantly blue, his mouth…

Please, God, don't let me faint, Abbie prayed despairingly. Not here, not now...

He was coming closer to her, Abbie recognised as she fought down the mingled feeling of panic and anger roaring through her. Too close. She mustn't let him see the effect he was having on her, or how much he was disturbing her, distressing her. She must, at all costs, appear calm and unmoved by his presence. She must.

He lifted his hand as though he was going to touch her, and without realising what she was doing Abbie was on her feet, backing away from him as she protested frantically. 'No...don't come any closer. Don't come near me...don't touch me...'

She knew that people were watching them, and that the restaurant had become oddly silent, but it hardly seemed to matter.

She didn't care what other people saw or thought; all she cared about was stopping Sam from closing the distance between them.

She felt her right hip come into painful contact with the edge of the table as she backed away from him; she could hear the cutlery and the glasses rattling.

'You have no right to be here,' she heard herself whisper harshly. 'No right at all...'

'Abbie, we need to talk...'

How calm and controlled his voice sounded in contrast to her own. Her brain registered these facts but her emotions couldn't react to them. The fact that almost everybody in the restaurant was watching them—her— a fact which normally would have been more than enough to make her grit her teeth and refuse to show any kind of emotion at all—just didn't seem to matter.

She had heard of people having panic attacks but had never really understood what that entailed. Now, suddenly, she did. Whilst her brain recognised that she was overreacting, that she was out of control, it was impossible for her to do anything about it, to hide what she was feeling.

'Don't come near me. I hate you,' she heard herself whisper dryly as she edged past him and turned towards the door. But it wasn't hatred that was making her heart pound so frantically, nor her body tremble so much. She had never known such fear, such shock, such panic.

As she stumbled into the reception area she saw Dennis coming towards her, his expression alert and anxious.

'Abbie, what is it? What's wrong?' she heard him asking in concern.

But she ignored the hand he put out to restrain her, shaking her head and telling him disjointedly, 'I...I don't feel well. I have to go home...I...'

'Let me drive you. Wait here and I'll get my car...'

'No,' she denied sharply. 'No, please...just...I'll be all right once I get home. I just need to be by myself,' she told him shakily. 'I'm sorry, Dennis...'

Unable to say any more, she turned on her heel and hurried towards the exit.

Her car was in the car park but she was in no fit state to drive. Fortunately it was still quite light, light enough at least for her to be able to take the footpath which ran through the fields and came out halfway down the lane to her small cottage.

The cottage was one of a pair which had originally been farmworkers' homes.

When Abbie had bought it her friends had thought she was mad to buy somewhere so far out of town and in such a run-down state. Now those same friends talked enviously of her foresight. The cottage had a very large garden, which Abbie had spent years and an awful lot of her spare time turning into a dream of a cottage garden. The house itself had been skilfully extended—the most recent addition being the pretty conservatory Abbie had added the previous summer.

She could almost hear the sound of her own frantic heartbeat as she hurried along the footpath. Every now and then she turned to look back over her shoulder, half afraid that he...that Sam might have followed her.

What was he doing here? What did he *want*? How long had he been sitting in the restaurant watching her? There was nothing for him here. *Nothing*...and no one.

No one...except...

She stopped moving, her body going very still.

'I think I saw Dad today,' Cathy had told her. She could almost hear the words now, see the expression on her daughter's face.

'No,' she whispered, unaware that the word sounded like a keening cry of despair as the wind took it and tossed it towards the empty sky. 'No. She's mine... You didn't want her. She's mine...'

As Abbie opened her front door she could hear her telephone ringing, but she couldn't bear to answer it. What if it was him—Sam? But why should *he* ring her? How could he have her number? He couldn't have come back because of anything to do with her or Cathy, she tried to reassure herself. It was just some horrible coincidence, that was all. He had probably been as shocked to see her in the restaurant as she had him.

But *he* hadn't looked shocked. He had looked... Abbie closed her eyes, not wanting to remember the way he had studied her, his gaze lingering on her eyes, her mouth, her body.

What had he thought when he'd seen her, a woman now and not a young girl any more? Had he looked at her and wondered why on earth he had ever desired her? Could he even remember that he *had* desired her, or had there been so many women in his life since then that he could no longer remember what it had felt like to hold her…to touch her…to…?

'No,' Abbie protested, her voice a rusty, unfamiliar sound of anguish in the empty room as she gripped hold of the worktop, willing the memories…the pain to subside.

It had been years since she had last thought about how it had felt to want Sam and to be wanted by him in return, and yet now, in the space of half a dozen hours, she had relived just how it had felt—not once but twice. And on both occasions her memories had been so sharp, so vivid, so devastating that she was still in shock from her defencelessness against them.

Why, when she had not thought about him like that in years, when she had deliberately refused to allow herself to remember those things about him which had once brought her such intense physical pleasure—because they were, after all, a fiction, a stupid self-delusion— should she so suddenly and so clearly be able to remember not just what it had felt like to have his mouth caressing hers, but also how he had smelt, how he had tasted, how the roughness of his jaw had felt beneath her fingertips, how he had…?

Her chest felt tight and full of pain, constricting her breathing, and her eyes burned and ached. She lifted her hand to rub them and realised to her horror that her face was wet and that she was crying.

What was happening to her? Why was she overreacting like this? Was it the shock of seeing him coming so quickly on top of finding her wedding dress and remembering?

She tensed as she heard a car drawing up outside. What if it was him? What if he had followed her? But it was Cathy's feet she could hear tapping on the stones outside, Cathy's voice tense with anxiety she could hear calling out to her.

She reached quickly for some kitchen towel to dry her wet face and tried to compose herself, but it was already too late. Cathy was hurrying into the kitchen, her face shadowed with pain and apprehension.

'You've seen him, haven't you?' she asked Abbie. 'You've seen Dad at the hotel.'

Abbie stared at her daughter, noting her heightened colour and guilty expression.

'You knew he would be there,' she whispered in disbelief. 'You knew and yet you said nothing. But how, why…?'

Abbie had started to cry again.

'Oh, Mum, I'm so sorry. I didn't… I never…'

Stuart had followed Cathy into the room and now he came over to her, putting his arm protectively around his fiancée as he told Abbie quietly, 'None of this has anything to do with Cathy, Abbie. At least not directly. *She's* not the one who is responsible for your ex-husband's return. I am.'

'You?' Abbie stared at him in confusion.

'Stuart only told me what he'd done today, when I happened to mention that I thought I'd seen Dad,' Cathy burst out. 'He wanted it to be a surprise.'

'Darling, why don't you let me explain?' Stuart suggested, kissing Cathy gently before turning back to Abbie.

'I know that Cathy would never tell you this herself—she loves you too much and she'd be too afraid of hurting you—but I know how much she has always wanted to meet her father—which, as my own parents have both said, is only natural.

'Cathy told me that she felt it was impossible for her to try to get in touch with him because she was afraid of hurting you, but it's over twenty years now since you divorced him, and I knew how much it would mean to Cathy to meet her father…to perhaps even have him here when we get married…and so I've been making a few discreet enquiries, trying to locate him.

'I had planned to fly out to Australia myself—meet him, talk with him. But…' Stuart gave a small shrug. 'Well, it seems he had ideas of his own. Believe me, the last thing I wanted to happen was for him just to turn up here.'

'You mean *you're* the one responsible for bringing him back?' Abbie demanded through semi-numb lips as she stared at Stuart.

'Yes,' he agreed.

'Having no doubt first fully discussed this plan of yours with your parents?' Abbie demanded cuttingly.

At her side she could see Cathy wince and smother a small protest, and it hurt her to see the way her daughter turned not to her but to Stuart for support, almost as though she was actually afraid of her mother, almost as though they were on opposing sides.

'Yes, as a matter of fact I did,' Stuart agreed woodenly.

'And they doubtless thought it was an excellent idea. Your mother fully approved of this plan, I imagine. You rely a great deal on your mother's approval, don't you, Stuart?' she asked with acid sweetness.

She could see that the tips of his ears were burning a dark, angry red, and an inner voice was warning her not to go any further, not to alienate her daughter completely by humiliating the man she loved, but Abbie refused to listen to it.

'Well, I am *Cathy's* mother, and if *I* thought it would benefit Cathy to meet her father you can be sure that *I* would have ensured that she did so.'

'Would you?' Stuart challenged angrily. 'You're so filled with your own hatred of him that you can't even see what's under your nose. Your own feelings are so important to you that you never even thought properly about what Cathy's feelings might be, about the fact that she might *need* to know her father, to meet him, to talk to him.

'You can't even see that Cathy's too afraid of hurting you, too anxious to protect you, to tell you how much she wants to know him.'

Abbie turned to look at her daughter.

'Cathy, is this true?' she demanded painfully.

Cathy's expression gave her her answer.

'*Why* have you never told me...said something?' she whispered.

'I...I didn't want to hurt you...'

'She knew you wouldn't understand,' Stuart informed Abbie brutally. 'And she knew as well that you wouldn't even allow her to have such feelings, to be curious about him, to want to know him—to do anything other than share your own bitterness.

'All you've ever told Cathy about her father is how he deserted you both. How he wasn't fit to be her father. How do you think that made her feel—to know how much you hated someone who was actually part of herself...?'

'I just wanted to protect you,' Abbie whispered to Cathy. 'I didn't want you to be hurt by him as... Oh, Cathy...' Abbie reached out to hug her daughter, and then froze in shock as Cathy retreated from her, turning instead into Stuart's arms.

'I'm sorry about all this, Mum,' she whispered, 'but what Stuart says is true. I *did* want to see my father, to meet him, to know him... You mustn't blame Stuart for what's happened...he just wanted to make me happy.'

She raised her face towards her fiancé's and smiled tearfully at him.

'He's only just told me about trying to find my father. He wanted to bring us together.'

'You had no right to interfere,' Abbie protested to Stuart, still in shock.

'I had every right,' Stuart contradicted her flatly. 'I love Cathy and I want her to be happy, and if meeting her father is what she wants—'

'It might be what she wants,' Abbie interrupted him, 'but as for it making her happy…' She stopped.

'I know all those years ago that he didn't want me, that he refused to believe I was his child,' Cathy told her gently, 'but times change, Mum. People change…'

'Some people may do,' Abbie agreed bitterly, 'but I'm not one of them. I haven't changed.'

'You loved him once,' Cathy reminded her tremulously.

'I thought I loved him,' Abbie corrected her sharply, 'and I thought that he loved me—but I was wrong. On both counts.'

CHAPTER FIVE

'SO TELL me again what happened,' Fran commanded. 'God, it's at times like this that I wish I'd never given up smoking...' She gave a heartfelt sigh.

Abbie gave her a wry look.

'I've already told you—twice.'

'I know, and I still can't believe it.'

They were sitting in Fran's kitchen, either side of the large pine table in the middle of the room.

'You mean that Stuart was trying to make a few discreet enquiries about Sam to try and track him down and then he suddenly turned up here out of the blue without any warning?'

'Apparently, if Stuart's to be believed,' Abbie told her grimly, her face crumpling as she admitted, 'Oh, Fran, I still can't take it in. Why, why has Cathy never said anything to *me* about wanting to meet him?' She drew a deep breath as she saw the compassion in her best friend's eyes.

'You think the same as Stuart and his damned mother, don't you?' she accused. 'You think that Cathy was too afraid to tell me...and that I was too full of my own feelings, my own needs, to be aware of what Cathy might want.'

'I don't think it's as clear-cut as all that,' Fran told her gently. 'Of course I understand why you feel the way you do, Abbie. Any mother would—just wait until Cathy has children of her own—but logically I can see why Cathy should be curious about him. It's a natural instinct in a child to want to know his or her parents.

73

'I *do* understand how *you* feel, Abbie,' she said, gently stretching out to cover her friend's hand with her own. 'Don't forget, I was there—even if I was only on the fringe of things at the time. I saw what the break-up of your marriage did to you, but…'

'But what?' Abbie challenged her.

'Sam did try to get in touch with you so that the two of you could talk,' she reminded Abbie gently. 'You said so yourself at the time, and he wanted to make financial provision for you both.'

'To talk…what about?' Abbie demanded. 'About how positive he was that Cathy couldn't possibly be his child and how sure he was that I must be having an affair with someone else?'

'It must have been a terrible shock for him when you told him that you were pregnant,' Fran suggested gently. 'Especially in those days. Now we know so much more about the results of such operations; we know that there *is* a very small risk of a woman who has been sterilised becoming pregnant or a man who has had a vasectomy fathering a child. But back then… And you have to remember that in Sam's case his shock must have been compounded by his guilt. To see you so obviously thrilled and excited at the thought of having a child when he knew, or thought he knew, that he could not give you one. You've said yourself that having a family wasn't something you'd ever really discussed.'

'You think I was wrong, don't you, Fran? If he'd just said that he couldn't understand how I had conceived,' Abbie blurted out, her normally strictly controlled emotions overwhelming her, 'then perhaps we could have talked it through. But to accuse me of having an affair—and with Lloyd—when he knew… I'd never had sex with anyone but him, Fran.'

She looked away from her friend and added in a low, reluctant voice, 'I still never have.'

As she looked back at her friend she could see that her admission had surprised her.

'What did you imagine?' she mocked her, with a return to her normal slightly acerbic manner. 'That I've had a secret sex life of unimaginable debauchery?' She shook her head. 'I've never wanted sex enough for it to be an appetite I could satisfy without a very deep emotional bond with my partner, and I've...since Sam I...'

'Life's not very fair to our sex, is it? Technically we're given the freedom to indulge our sexual appetites without the risk of an unwanted pregnancy, without the economic need to find ourselves a mate to support us, but in nine out of ten cases our emotions let us down every time.'

'Try not to be too hard on Stuart and Cathy,' Fran warned her quietly. 'I'm sure that Stuart believes he acted from the best of motives. He's young and he's very much in love. He probably can't see beyond his desire to make Cathy happy...'

'His desire to make Cathy happy?' Abbie asked her tiredly. 'Or his mother's desire to meddle? Oh, I'm sorry,' she apologised, closing her eyes and lifting her hand to rub her aching neck muscles. 'I just don't know what's happening to me these days, Fran. But ever since Cathy and Stuart got engaged I feel as if...as though...'

'As though you're losing her?' Fran suggested softly.

Abbie flushed slightly and avoided looking at her before admitting gruffly, 'It's ridiculous, I know, for me to feel jealous because my daughter's fallen in love, because there's someone in her life who's now more important to her than I am. I keep telling myself that I'm overreacting, reminding myself that to all intents and purposes Cathy had already left home before she met

Stuart, that it's only natural that Stuart's mother wants to help with the organisation of the wedding, and yet, at the same time, deep down inside I feel hurt and resentful and, yes, pushed out…redundant…

'It's not just that Cathy doesn't seem to need me any more, but that she doesn't seem to want me either—it's as if I'm a nuisance, a burden, as if I'm standing in the way of her new life. And Stuart's family can give her so much more than I can, Fran. Every time I see Stuart's mother I can almost see her thinking what a poor mother I am, congratulating herself on her own superiority. And, of course, because Stuart thinks she's wonderful, Cathy also—'

'Cathy loves you,' Fran interrupted her calmly. 'And if you want my opinion I suspect that Stuart's mother feels rather intimidated by you and by what you've achieved, Abbie. Yes, she's fulfilling the traditional matriarchal role in her family, but she's never had to go out and prove herself as you have done. I'm not being unkind, but it's no secret locally that both her family and Stuart's father's have always been pretty comfortably off. Materially, she's never wanted for anything, never had to worry…and she's certainly never had to even think about having to support herself. And as for her own family life…

'Well, she and I are both members of the same committee. She's the chairperson and I'm one of the lowliest of the low, but I have heard whispers of gossip that there was a time when her eldest daughter did rather rebel against the kind of mothering that some people prefer to call smothering. Personally, the mere fact that she's even suggested taking over the planning of the wedding suggests to me an incredible lack of tact, but it isn't Stuart's mother that really bothers you, is it?'

'No,' Abbie admitted. 'It's Cathy. She seems to have changed so much since she and Stuart fell in love…'

'She's growing up, Abbie, establishing her own identity and her independence, and you forget sometimes that the role model you've given her, with all that you've achieved, is a pretty tough challenge for her to try to meet, never mind match.'

'I did what I did because I had to, not because I wanted to,' Abbie protested. 'Given the choice, the chance, there was nothing I would have wanted more than to be a proper stay-at-home mother, to have a big family, to give Cathy brothers and sisters…a father…' she added in a strained whisper.

'You *are* a proper mother,' Fran assured her firmly. 'You've worked so hard, Abbie, to build up your business. I can remember the days when you had three different part-time jobs in order to support Cathy and yourself, and yet you still managed to spend time with her, give her more time than many full-time mothers. And look at the way you mother everyone who works for you. You've got a mothering instinct a mile wide, and if I had a pound for every time my two complain that they wish I was more like you I'd be a very wealthy woman.'

'Why did Sam have to come back, Fran?' Abbie returned to the problem uppermost in her mind. 'Why couldn't he just have left us alone? I'm so afraid, Fran.' She gave a little shiver. 'Afraid that I'm going to lose Cathy for good, and yet I can't…I can't change my feelings…how I *still* feel about Sam…'

'Why don't you tell Cathy what you've told me?' Fran suggested softly to her. 'I'm sure when she understands—'

'I can't,' Abbie interrupted her fiercely. 'If I do she'll think that I'm trying to put emotional pressure on her not to see her father, and it's obvious that she does want to see him…'

'You know what you need, don't you?' Fran told her firmly. 'You need a bit of romantic interest of your own in your life—a relationship.'

'A relationship? What on earth for?' Abbie scoffed. 'Don't you think my life has enough complications in it already?'

'Well, for one thing, if I were in your shoes I should find it rather ego-boosting to face a man I once loved and who once hurt me very badly with another man at my side, to show him and the rest of the world that he doesn't matter to me any more. And for another… Well, let's just say that it's high time you started rounding out your life a little bit more and taking advantage of the unfair natural advantages you have over the rest of us. I promise you, if I were single and I had your looks, I wouldn't be sitting at home every night on my own.'

'No?' Abbie queried dryly. 'And where, pray tell me, am I supposed to find this man…this relationship?'

'Well, I could always lend you Lloyd to practise on,' Fran told her mischievously. 'Now, that would set the cat amongst the pigeons and set your Sam wondering…'

'He is *not* my Sam,' Abbie reminded her. 'And as for him doing any wondering about my personal relationships with members of his sex, or lack of them—I doubt that he'd care one way or the other.'

'Do you want him to?' Fran asked her.

Abbie gave her an angry look. 'No, of course I don't—how could I? The only thing I want from Sam is for him to disappear.'

An hour later Abbie was on her way home, having first called to collect her car from the hotel car park and assure Dennis that, yes, she was perfectly all right and fully recovered, and then made a second call to the small office she rented in the high street to check with her assistant and see if there were any urgent matters she needed to attend to.

Her face burned a little as she remembered Dennis's concerned enquiries. Even though he hadn't actually witnessed what had happened for himself, she knew he must have heard about it from those who had. Of all the things, large and small, she had regretted doing in her life, her failure to conceal her shock at seeing Sam last night currently came top of the list.

But surely Sam would not have the gall to imagine her shocked reaction might have been because she was still nursing a broken heart over him? He must know exactly how she felt about him, how fierce and deep her hatred ran. After all, she had made it plain enough all those years ago when he had had the audacity, the sheer heart-wrenching inability to guess what he was doing to her, to try and suggest that they attempt to resolve their differences.

Her parents had gently suggested that it might be best if she *did* talk to him, and she remembered how hurt and upset she had been that they could even think such a thing.

Were doubts about paternity to happen today, of course, things would be different: there were DNA tests which could be taken to prove beyond doubt the identity of the father of a child. But she was glad that such an option had not been open to her. The last thing she would have wanted was to feel that a man was accepting paternity of her child begrudgingly and reluctantly.

She swallowed fiercely as she turned the car into her drive and switched off the engine. It was a pity that her parents were away visiting friends in the Dordogne; they would have understood how she felt.

Gathering up her handbag and the post she had collected from the office, she headed for the back door, keys at the ready—only when she inserted them she discovered that the door was already unlocked.

Frowning, she stepped forward uncertainly, her body tensing slightly, and opened the door. Only she and Cathy had keys for the house. Did that mean that her daughter had perhaps been having second thoughts?

As she stepped into the kitchen Abbie came to an abrupt halt. It wasn't Cathy who was sitting in one of the pretty patchwork-cushioned chairs, talking to the purring cat who had removed herself from her customary bed beside the Aga and climbed onto his knee, but Sam.

Gently dislodging the cat, he stood up, watching her unsmilingly.

Hugging her letters and bag as fiercely to her body as though they were a lifeline, Abbie demanded furiously, 'What are you doing here? How did you get in?'

'Cathy loaned me her keys,' he told her quietly, then added in a voice that was markedly calm in contrast to her own shocked fury, but still ominously determined for all that, 'We need to talk.'

Standing up to his full height here in her kitchen, with less than three feet between them, he seemed very much taller and bigger than he had done last night. But then she was wearing flat shoes, Abbie recognised. It irked her that he should appear so calmly and comfortably at home in her own house whilst she felt so on edge and caught off guard, but then he would have done that deliberately, knowing that she wouldn't be expecting him, knowing that her shock would give him the edge over her...the advantage.

There were two ways she could deal with this, she decided. Either passively, by refusing to say or do anything and simply walking away from him, or with aggression, by letting him know that there was nothing, *nothing* he could say or do that could ever change her feelings or her determination to keep him out of their lives. *Their* lives…

Passivity had never been her strong suit, she acknowledged. She preferred action.

'*We* need to talk?' she queried coldly. 'Since when did *you* have the right to claim to know what I may or may not need, Sam?' She gave him an icy smile. '*You* may wish to talk to *me*, but I assure you I have no desire and certainly no need to talk to you.'

'We need to talk. Not for our own sakes,' Sam continued, as though she simply hadn't spoken, 'but for our daughter's.'

'*Our* daughter's?' Abbie nearly choked on her fury as she glared at him. '*You* have no daughter,' she spat at him. 'Cathy is *mine*, all mine. You didn't want her. You denied that you could ever have fathered her… remember?'

'I made a mistake. I was wrong. I didn't realise then…'

Abbie continued to stare at him, the blood draining out of her face as the shock of what he was saying made her body tremble.

She hadn't realised until now how much she had been depending on him rejecting Cathy for a second time.

'No,' she whispered in a paper-thin voice. 'Cathy isn't your child,' she denied. 'Cathy is my child. She's always been mine. She never—'

'She never what? She never wanted to know anything about me, to have anything to do with me? She hates me as much as you do? Those are *your* feelings, not Cathy's, Abbie,' he told her sternly, shaking his head whilst Abbie's heart turned over in anguish at the easy way in which Cathy's name had slipped off his tongue, as though for all the world he were used to saying it, as though he had been calling her Cathy, his Cathy, from the day of her birth and not...

'Cathy got in touch with me, not the other way round,' he reminded her, but Abbie wouldn't let him continue.

'Cathy did *not* get in touch with you. It was Stuart who interfered, who assumed he had the right—'

'To what? To make Cathy happy?' He gave her a derisive look. 'But you don't think that anyone has the right or the ability to make Cathy happy other than you, do you, Abbie? In fact, you don't think that even Cathy has the right to say what makes her happy.'

'That's not true,' Abbie denied angrily, her face flushing hotly at his accusation. 'Cathy is twenty-two, an adult, and—'

'And what?' Sam pressed her.

Like her, he was dressed casually, but she was irritably conscious of the fact that, though a pair of black leggings topped off with a chunky oatmeal outsize sweater might feel comfortable and practical, they did not look anything like as good on her small frame as Sam's faded and well-worn jeans and soft checked shirt looked on his lean, hard-muscled body.

It was ridiculous that a man of his age should still have such a formidably male-looking body—his stomach flat and taut, his rear, from the side view she had of it, enviably taut and muscular... Abbie hastily looked away from him. What on earth was the matter with her? Men's backsides, taut and muscular or not, were of no interest whatsoever to her—especially this man's, most especially this man's—even if now...

'And what?' she asked tiredly, throwing the question back at Sam, her hands straying betrayingly to her neck and the aching muscles there which gave away her growing tension.

'Cathy is a woman,' Sam persisted. 'You admit that, but you don't treat her as one. You don't allow her to have her own feelings, her own needs. You don't allow her to even tell you that she would like to meet me…'

'Did she?' Abbie swallowed. 'Did Cathy tell *you* that?'

'No. Not in so many words. But she did tell me—'

'You've spoken to her?' Abbie interrupted him swiftly.

'Yes, she and Stuart came to see me this morning. We had a long discussion, cleared up certain misconceptions…'

'What misconceptions,' Abbie demanded, a cold, warning sensation gripping her body unpleasantly.

'Misconceptions such as the fact that I have supposedly spent the last twenty-two years refusing to accept the fact that I have a daughter, that I haven't felt either guilt or pain about the fact that initially I couldn't accept that she was my child. Misconceptions about the reasons why I felt unable to be the one to make contact with her, even though there were many, many times when I wanted to do so.'

'You're lying,' Abbie told him fiercely. 'You're just saying that now because…'

'Because what?' he invited her.

'Why have you come here? What do you want?' Abbie demanded, changing tack.

'I came here because I learned that someone from England was making enquiries about me,' he told her promptly. 'And as for what I want, I don't think it would be a very good idea if I answered that question right now. You aren't in the mood to hear what I want to say.'

'I'll never be in the right mood to listen to anything

you have to say other than goodbye,' Abbie told him bitterly. 'And I've already heard you say that.'

'No, Abbie, you haven't,' he corrected her. '*You* were the one who said goodbye to me—or rather the one who walked out on me.'

Abbie stared at him.

'Because you'd accused me of trying to pass another man's child off as yours... Because you'd deceived me by never even bothering to tell me that you'd had a vasectomy—and, by the way, men who have had vasectomies *do* still produce children.'

'Yes, I know,' Sam agreed. 'And I also know that almost invariably they react to the initial news that they have done in the same way that I did. Most partners of such men find that they want to have medical proof that he is actually the father of their child before the man can accept it.

'I'm not alone in reacting the way I did, Abbie. That doesn't make it right, I know that, and it doesn't lessen the pain and shock I know you must have felt. But I felt pain and shock as well, you know. The pain and shock of believing the woman I was deeply and helplessly in love with had betrayed me with another man. At twenty-six I might have seemed adult and mature to you, but I wasn't—not inside. Men don't mature as quickly as women and I was still immature enough to get infernally jealous, and to feel very, very insecure about the strength of your love for me. You were so young...'

'But not too young to leave alone, expecting your baby,' Abbie told him bitterly.

Immediately Sam's eyes darkened, his jaw hardening in betrayal of his emotions.

'I did not leave you alone,' he denied harshly. 'I was the one who wanted to try for a reconciliation—remember? I wasn't the one who refused to accept a penny,

who said that they'd rather die than have an allowance
from me...'

'I didn't want your money,' Abbie stormed, infuriated
by his apparent inability, even after all these years, to
see what an insult she had felt it was to her that he
should calmly offer to support her and a baby he refused
to admit was his—as though she was some...some cast-
off bit on the side, some...some... 'I wanted—' She
stopped abruptly, blinking hard to dissipate the angry
tears she could feel building at the back of her eyes.

'You wanted what?' Sam pressed her.

'I wanted nothing. Nothing...' Abbie bit out venom-
ously at him. 'Just to have you out of my life...our lives.
You might have decided to accept now that you are
Cathy's father, but so far as I am concerned—'

'You'll never forgive me?' Sam supplied grimly for
her.

There was an expression in his eyes that caused Abbie
a small twinge of alarm, a warning that she was pushing
him to the limits of his patience and temper. But she
chose to ignore it. Why should she care about his feelings? After all, when had he ever cared about hers?

'Never,' she agreed vehemently, adding for good
measure, 'You might have managed to convince, to deceive Cathy into believing that you regret what happened, but you can't deceive me—not a second time.
When did it happen, this change of heart, this discovery
that you might have been wrong?' she jeered tauntingly.
'Last week...last month...? Did you open your eyes one
morning and after years of never even giving her a second thought suddenly decide you wanted to see her?'

'No,' Sam denied quietly.

There was a small pulse beating under the taut flesh
of his throat and Abbie found that she couldn't drag her
gaze away from it. Apart from the ominous tightening

of his jaw, and a certain look in his eyes, it was the only sign he had given that he was not totally, calmly and completely in control of his emotions and the situation.

It pleased her to know that she had the power to anger him, to get under his skin.

'Whether you choose to believe it or not, Abbie, the truth is that there has never been a day, never been a night when I have not thought about…her. When I have not wished that things could have been different. Initially, that wish was quite simply that there could have been some way in which I could have believed that she was my child, and then later, when I discovered that there was a chance that she could be…'

Abbie saw his chest expand as he took a deep breath.

'I'm not going to indulge your desire for revenge by detailing the guilt and anguish that I suffered, the regret…'

'No,' Abbie agreed dryly. 'I shouldn't if I were you. Save it for someone stupid enough to believe you, Sam, because I certainly don't. If you genuinely did feel any of those emotions, why didn't you try to contact us…Cathy…then?'

'Because I didn't think it was fair…I didn't feel I had the right,' he told her simply. 'And besides…'

'Besides what?' Abbie scoffed. For some reason his quiet, sad words were hurting her, making her feel… making her wish… 'Besides, you were too involved in your own life, your own relationships? Did you ever marry again, Sam?'

'No,' he told her curtly, turning his head away from her. And then, looking straight at her, he added slowly, 'And I haven't fathered any more children either, which is why—'

'You've now decided you want to take up your fifty per cent option on Cathy?' Abbie taunted him.

'No,' he told her quietly. 'The reason I came back, virtually the only reason I came back, is because Cathy wanted to meet me. I have no rights where she is concerned. My emotions, my needs must always come second to hers. Had she never made any move to contact me I would have left matters as they stood, but since she has—'

'Since *Stuart* has,' Abbie interrupted fiercely. 'It was *Stuart* who wanted to find you, Sam, not Cathy.'

'What is it you're afraid of, Abbie?' he challenged her quietly. 'Letting Cathy discover that I'm not perhaps the villain you've always painted me? That my mistake, my error, was one of vulnerability and humanity rather than deliberate cruelty, as she seems to have been told?'

'No, that's not true,' Abbie denied. 'I just wanted to protect her, to stop her from being hurt.'

'By telling her that I didn't want her...? Did you ever tell her how much I wanted *you*, Abbie,' he asked her softly, sliding the question under her guard and aiming at her heart with all the dexterity of a surgeon with a knife.

As the pain pierced her Abbie gave a small, instinctive cry of protest, closing her eyes against the expression she could see in his face.

'Did you tell her how much I loved you? How much you loved me, how you wanted me?' he pressed, refusing to release her from her agony. 'Did you tell her how she was conceived—how, when we made love, you cried out to me in pleasure and ecstasy? How you begged me to fill and possess you completely, to take you and make you for ever my own? Did you tell her any of *these* things, Abbie, to balance the rest of what you felt it necessary to tell her?'

'I told her everything she needed to know,' Abbie said harshly.

She was breathing too fast and too shallowly; her heart was thumping and her legs felt shakily weak. She desperately wanted to sit down, but Sam was standing between her and the chairs. Even so, she made an instinctive move towards one of them, terrified that if she stayed where she was the weakness she could feel threatening her would totally overcome her. But her movements were slow and clumsy, and instead of stepping past Sam she somehow collided with him.

The unexpected impact of his body against her own drove the air from her lungs, leaving her breathing in quick panic, her hands pushing frantically at his chest to distance herself from him even though all he had done was to put out an arm to steady her.

Abbie could see him frowning as he looked down at her. Panic started to explode inside her as her body began to recognise and react to the familiarity of his.

To her horror, Abbie could feel her breasts swelling and hardening as they made contact with the warmth of his body. Beneath the hand she had put out to ward him off she could feel the springy thickness of his body hair underneath his shirt.

Appalled by what was happening to her, Abbie froze. She could feel his heart beating, smell the unforgettably male scent of him, see the shadow on his jaw where he'd shaved, the small mole tucked just inside his collar, which she had once teased and kissed and...

Despairingly she closed her eyes, trying to blot him out, but instantly so many shocking images and memories danced beneath her shuttered eyelids that she immediately opened them again, her mouth forming a small protesting denial.

'Let me go,' she demanded. 'Let me...'

'You're the one holding onto me, Abbie,' Sam informed her, and as she looked down at where her fingers were locked in the fabric of his shirt Abbie realised that it was true. She could feel the hot blood burning up under her skin, covering her whole body in a scarlet tide of mortification.

'I'm still a man,' he added warningly as he looked down at her, 'even if I am older, and I'm still liable to react exactly the same way as I always did to the feel of your breasts pressing against my body, and the look in your eyes that means that you want me to kiss you...and more...'

'No,' Abbie denied, furious. 'No. Never. I hate you. I...' She gave a small yelp of protest as Sam secured her against his body with one arm and then slid his free hand along her jaw and into her hair, tilting her face up towards his own, not giving her time to renew her verbal assault on him as he lowered his head and covered her half-open mouth with his own.

It shouldn't have been possible for him to get any response out of her. There wasn't *any* way she had the remotest scrap of feeling left for him other than loathing. She was a woman now, not an inexperienced, easily impressed girl whose emotions and sexuality could be aroused at will by a man who had managed to convince her that he loved and wanted her.

No. It shouldn't have been possible at all. So why... why, instead of instantly repudiating him, did her mouth, her body soften so immediately against his? Why did her lips cling almost beseechingly to his? Why did her heart start to pound in frantic excitement at the familiar delicate stroke of his tongue against her lips? Why? Why? Why was she pressing herself closer and closer to him, straining, aching, yearning for the feel of his skin against her own?

In the distance Abbie could hear someone moaning softly as Sam's tongue stroked rhythmically in and out of her mouth. His hand slid down her back to press her hips into his body, and as the movement of his pelvis imitated the sensual thrust of his tongue her body melted, yielded to the sensual mastery of his.

She was trembling from head to foot, unable to control her reactions to him, and she recognised in shock that the moaning she could hear was her own. Sam's hand moved up her body, gently stroking the outside of her breast. Once that had been a signal between them that he wanted to touch her more intimately, to remove her clothing and stroke and caress her breasts, to suckle gently on their small pink tips until she twisted frantically beneath his hands and breathlessly begged him for more.

She could feel the flat pad of his thumb rubbing against her nipple, and she could feel, as well, its instant aching response to him.

Abruptly she froze. What on earth was she doing?

'Let go of me,' she demanded furiously, wrenching her mouth and her body away from him and then almost childishly wiping her hand across her mouth, as though she was trying to wipe away the taste and feel of him, before saying huskily, 'I detest you so much that…'

'That you want me to take you to bed just so that you can prove it to me?' Sam suggested harshly.

Abbie stared at him in shock, her body slowly filling with pain.

'You had no right to touch me like that,' she told him sickly, all the fight suddenly leaving her. 'No right at all.'

She turned away from him and started to walk back to the table, stiffening as she heard him saying her name.

'Cathy had no right to give you her keys, either,' she added shakily. 'This is *my* home and I don't want you in it.'

'She gave them to me because she felt it was the only way you'd ever agree to talk to me,' Sam told her.

'Talk?' Abbie turned to face him, her eyes brilliant with the angry shamed tears she couldn't hide. 'What is there for us to talk about? We've already said it all, every damaging, destructive, hurting word we could possibly have to say. You're right. I can't stop Cathy from seeing you if she wants to. That's *her* choice and her right. But *I* have rights and choices too,' she told him, lifting her chin. 'And my right...*my* choice is that whatever there once was between us is over and finished, and I never want to see you again. Now, please go.'

For a moment she thought he was going to argue with her, and she prayed that her strength, her self-control would somehow hold out long enough for her to make him leave, but to her relief, after a brief pause, he turned towards the door, pausing to look at her for a long moment before actually going through it.

It was only after he had gone that she realised he still had her keys.

Never mind, she consoled herself, she could always have the locks changed.

The locks to her house, maybe, but the locks to her heart... Leaning her head on the table, she gave way to the tears she couldn't hold back any more.

CHAPTER SIX

'AND you'll never guess what.' Cathy's face was pink with excitement as she came rushing into the kitchen, giving her mother an absent hug before continuing, 'We think we've found a house, and Dad has offered to pay for the wedding breakfast. We were talking about it last night when we went back to the hotel with him.'

She pulled a small face. 'He still hasn't found anywhere to rent, although he did say that if he accepts this Chair they've offered him at the university—which he thinks he will—'

'What Chair?' Abbie demanded tightly as she fought to control her shock. Sam had said nothing to her about being offered a job at the university. 'I thought his visit was only going to be a temporary thing...'

'Well, it was,' Cathy agreed, suddenly looking slightly uncomfortable. 'But...well, it seems that he's been wanting to come home...to come back,' she amended hastily, 'for ages, and now that he and I...well... Well, I'm all the family he's got, and—'

'All the family he's got?' Abbie interrupted her indignantly. Cathy was *her* daughter.

'He *is* my father,' Cathy told her defensively, her eyes avoiding Abbie's, the sparkling look of excitement dying out of her eyes as she moved edgily around the kitchen.

It was a week now since Abbie had first seen Sam at the hotel, and she had had all the locks changed and pointedly told Cathy that she was not to give a new set of keys to her father.

She had told herself that she would simply have to

grit her teeth and ignore Sam's presence for the hope-
fully brief duration of his visit, and now, to discover that
not only was he involving himself in the arrangements
for Cathy's wedding but that he was also making plans
to move back permanently, she was thrown into a state
of confused emotions. The chief of which, or so she told
herself, was anger—a wholly justifiable anger, too, in
the circumstances.

'I thought you'd be pleased,' she heard Cathy telling
her almost challengingly. 'Oh, it's no use,' she finished
bitterly. 'Stuart said that you wouldn't understand, that
you wouldn't want to let go of your resentment against
Dad...'

'Stuart said—' Abbie snapped off the words and then
forced a deep breath before starting again. 'Tell me
about the house,' she invited, trying to find a less contentious topic of conversation. Perhaps later, when she
had calmed down a little, she might be able to talk more
rationally to Cathy about Sam's involvement with her
wedding.

'Oh, it's perfect,' Cathy told her enthusiastically, her
eyes starting to sparkle again, her voice light with relief.
'Three bedrooms, and it's got a huge private back garden. The kitchen and bathroom are pretty awful—' she
pulled a face '—but as Dad was saying when he saw
it—'

'Your father's already seen the house?' Abbie interrupted.

'Yes, we took him to see it last night. Well, it was on
his way to Charlesford. He had an appointment at the
university about this post he's been offered, and Stuart
said why didn't he come with us so that we could show
him the house. Stuart and Dad get on well together,'
Cathy added enthusiastically. 'Dad was telling Stuart
that his father used to be an accountant.'

'Really? Let's hope that that's all they've got in common,' Abbie couldn't resist saying acerbically. Although she regretted the comment almost as soon as she had uttered it when she saw the look of hurt withdrawal in Cathy's eyes.

'I...I'm sorry, darling,' she apologised huskily. 'It's just...'

'It doesn't matter, Mum,' Cathy told her quickly—too quickly? Abbie wondered sensitively as, without giving her the opportunity to explain or apologise properly, Cathy hurried on.

'I'm longing for you to see the house, only we can't show you until the weekend. It's empty, by the way, which is another plus point. We're taking Dad to meet Stuart's grandparents tomorrow evening, and then it's Julia's little girl's birthday party the day after and Mama Grimshaw is having the whole family round—'

'Including your father, no doubt?' Abbie interrupted through gritted teeth.

Cathy gave her an uncertain look.

'Well, yes, she has invited him. But how did you...?'

'I—'

'Look, Mum, I've got to go,' Cathy told her quickly. 'But one of the reasons I've called round is because Dad said that he wanted, that he *needed* to talk to you about the wedding reception. He said you'd probably got your own ideas about where it should be held...'

'Oh, he did, did he?' Abbie couldn't resist interjecting. After another quick, uncertain look at her, Cathy continued, 'I told him that he'd probably get you in any evening because you never really go out much. He seemed surprised.' Cathy laughed.   'He asked me if there was anyone special in your life...a man. I told him that you weren't really interested in men.

'Look, Mum...' Cathy paused and gave Abbie a

pleading look. 'When Dad does get in touch with you, you will be…nice to him, won't you? I do understand how you feel, but it's like Stuart said—I *am* only going to get married once and I so much want it all to be right… And what would make it so special for me would be to have you both there with me.' Her eyes filled with tears and Abbie's bitterness and anger suddenly melted.

'Of course it will be all right, and special. Very, very special—just like you,' she told Cathy emotionally, hugging her tightly.

Was it, after all, so much of a sacrifice to make? Her pride in exchange for her daughter's happiness on such a very important day? What mattered the most to her? There was really no contest, was there? Abbie acknowledged, which meant that when Sam did get in touch with her she would just have to remember that it was Cathy's feelings which must come first on this occasion, and not her own.

'Abbie.'

She recognised his voice immediately, even though it was distorted slightly by the telephone line: authoritative, compelling and oh, so sensually disturbing. She could actually feel the tiny hairs lifting on her arms as she gripped the receiver and responded jerkily, 'Yes, Sam?'

'I was wondering if we could meet to discuss this business of Cathy's wedding. I take it that she has mentioned my…?'

'She has told me that you've offered to pay for the reception,' Abbie agreed, her feelings getting the better of her as she added under her breath, 'Amongst other things…'

'What other things?' Sam probed, his hearing rather more acute than she had expected.

'The fact that you're apparently considering moving back here…back "home",' she emphasised with heavy irony. 'Why—?'

'Why didn't I tell you first?' Sam interrupted her, and continued before Abbie could tell him that that had not been what she had been about to say. 'You didn't really give me much opportunity, did you? And besides—'

'What you do with your life is none of my business,' Abbie finished grittily, before adding fiercely, 'Just as Cathy is none of yours.'

There, it was out. The words and the hostility she knew she had revealed with them exposed, in spite of all her good intentions not to quarrel with him for Cathy's sake.

'She is our daughter,' Sam pointed out quietly, adding, 'Look, I don't want to quarrel with you over this, Abbie.'

'*You* don't want to quarrel with *me*… Oh, I know *that*,' Abbie agreed bitterly. 'Just like I know that given the choice you'd rather not have anything to do with me at all. What you want, the person you want, is Cathy. Not me. Don't think I don't know that, Sam. I'm not a complete fool, you know…not any more.'

'No, you're wrong,' Sam told her grimly.

'Am I? Then why are you so determined to force your way into her life?' Abbie demanded scornfully. 'And don't try to tell me that that's not what you are doing. Why else would you offer to pay for her wedding reception? Why else have you come back here? Why else are you planning to move back here permanently? It has to be because of Cathy, Sam. There isn't any other logical reason.'

'No other logical reason, perhaps not,' Sam agreed, his voice suddenly oddly heavy, weary almost. 'But then where emotions are concerned none of us tend to behave very logically, do we?'

Abbie sniffed suspiciously.

'What are you trying to say?' she demanded.

'Is it really my presence in Cathy's life you are so antagonistic to?' Sam challenged her softly. 'Or do you fear that somehow that might involve me in your own? We're both adults, Abbie, and we both share a responsibility towards our daughter...'

Abbie caught her breath on a swift shock of anger at the barefaced injustice of his remark.

How *dared* he talk to her about responsibility? Him of all people!

'No matter what our private feelings are,' he continued firmly, 'it's Cathy's feelings that are paramount here. She wants us both to be at her wedding; she wants us both to be involved. She wants—'

'*I* know what Cathy wants,' Abbie interrupted him curtly.

'Then you'll agree that for her sake we need to meet— to discuss not only the wedding but also a way of finding some middle ground between us, at least until after the wedding is over.'

Abbie was suddenly too tired to argue any further, and besides, what was the point? She knew that he was right and she suspected that Cathy would never really forgive her if she didn't go along with her daughter's desire to have them both involved in her wedding.

'If you're free this evening I could come and pick you up,' she heard Sam saying, patently taking her silence for agreement. 'I thought it might be preferable from both our points of view if we were to talk in neutral surroundings. Unless—'

'Yes...yes, I agree,' Abbie cut in tiredly. 'But there's

no need for you to go to the trouble of picking me up.
I can meet you.'

'If that's what you prefer,' Sam agreed cordially.

As they arranged to meet, at a small local pub which
had a famously excellent restaurant, Abbie wondered
why she had expected Sam to try to persuade her to let
him pick her up, and why she felt so disquietingly dis-
appointed that he hadn't. Surely the last thing she
wanted was to spend any more time in his company than
was absolutely necessary?

'Eight o'clock, then,' she heard him saying.

'Eight o'clock,' she agreed.

Was a fine cream wool cocktail suit worn over a silky
camisole rather too over the top for a midweek meal in
a pub restaurant? Even if it did have the reputation locally as being one of *the* places to eat? Abbie wondered
soulfully as she studied her reflection in the mirror.

The Abbie of old would never have worn cream, considering it too dull and plain. The years hadn't just
brought a few fine lines around her eyes, she acknowledged, they had brought wisdom and a certain amount
of self-awareness as well.

Nowadays, she no longer needed her clothes to pro-
claim her self-confidence for her.

Cream suited her. The suit's fluid easy lines hinted
subtly at the curves of her figure rather than hugging
them, and if the skirt, which ended at mid-calf, had
caused Cathy to wrinkle her nose and complain that it
was too long, then the long slit which divided the back
was more than enough to prove that it wasn't any need
to keep her legs hidden from view which had led to her
choice of outfit.

Plain gold earrings—a Christmas present to herself the
year Cathy graduated and she'd been invited to join the

local Chamber of Commerce for the first time—and the briefest touch of a new perfume she had fallen for on an infrequent day out in London. A final glance in the mirror to check that her eyeshadow was immaculately discreet and that her lipstick did not make her look as though she was pouting, waiting to be kissed, and she was ready.

A small, bleak expression crossed her face. There had been a time when the knowledge that the lipstick she was so carefully trying to apply was going to be kissed off by Sam had caused her hand to shake so much with excitement—and not just her hand either, she acknowledged—that her attempts to apply it had inevitably been abandoned. It still hurt even now to remember how happy she had been, how much in love. Was *that* why she had responded to Sam's kiss? Did he know? Had he guessed that in all the years they had been apart no one...no one had aroused that kind of reaction in her?

How had *he* felt when he'd held her in his arms again? Had he, too, remembered how it had once been between them, or had he simply gloated over the fact that she was so unable to conceal her reaction to him? Had he been amused, gratified, his ego stroked by the knowledge that he could still arouse her?

Did he...Cathy...anyone really know or understand how she felt, just what an effort it was for her to see him...to try to behave rationally and calmly? Did Cathy really understand what she was asking of her, or did her daughter simply think that a woman of her mother's age was past feeling the acute sharpness of emotions she considered the exclusive province of the young?

Emotions... What emotions? Abbie asked herself angrily. The only emotion she felt or wanted to feel towards her ex-husband was one of loathing. That was the only emotion he deserved from her.

* * *

The publican, who was one of her clients, welcomed her with a warm smile as she walked into the busy cocktail bar.

Sam was already there, and Abbie could see him watching them as Jeff gazed appreciatively at her, his conversation that of one business colleague to another but his eyes saying that she was a woman whom he found very, very attractive.

Sam, who had stood up as she entered the bar, put down the glass he was holding and began walking purposefully towards them, leaving Abbie with no option other than to introduce the two men. She could see the speculative interest in Jeff's eyes—and the male envy—and so, she recognised, could Sam. She supposed she ought to feel pleased that he was being made aware of the fact that other men still found her attractive, especially in view of what Cathy had told him, but she felt far too tense and on edge to want to play power-games.

'Would you like a drink or would you prefer to go straight to our table?' Sam asked her.

'Straight to the table,' Abbie responded.

As they were shown to their table she realised that the couple seated close to them were one of Stuart's sisters and her husband. As she acknowledged their smiles Abbie told herself grimly that there was no necessity for her to introduce Sam to them—after all, he would be meeting them soon enough.

She wasn't prepared to admit, even to herself, that it hurt knowing that *he* had been invited to Stuart's family party and she had not.

Not that she would have wanted to be invited, she denied to herself. Stuart's mother was someone she found it much easier to get on with at a distance, although she had kept her personal views on Cathy's future mother-in-law to herself, for Cathy's sake.

'You seem to be very well-known locally,' was Sam's comment as they sat down.

'I have a lot of business contacts,' Abbie agreed.

'And a very successful business,' Sam commented as the head waiter handed them their menus.

'You find that surprising?' Abbie couldn't resist challenging him.

'Not surprising…' he told her, after a small pause, leaving Abbie to probe.

'Not surprising, but…but what?'

For a moment she thought that he wasn't going to answer her, but then he closed the menu he had been studying and leaned across the table to tell her quietly, 'Not surprising, but humbling. That you possess the ability to make a success of your life doesn't surprise me. The raw material for that was always there, and despite all my other faults I hope I've never been the kind of man who can't recognise and appreciate an intelligent and courageous woman when I see one.

'No, your success doesn't surprise me, Abbie, neither does the way you've clung to your independence, bringing Cathy up on your own, giving her all the love and the security I know she must have had just by looking at her and watching her. Even the way you've clung to your…feelings about me doesn't surprise me. They all of them humble me and yet hurt me as well, because they reinforce the self-knowledge that *I* have made them necessary, that through *my* weakness you have had to develop your great strength.

'When Cathy first told me that there wasn't anyone…a man in your life, I was tempted not to believe her, but then I realised that what she said was probably true—and why... What, after all, could a man...any man...give you that you haven't obtained for yourself?'

He gave her an ironic look.

'Once, a long, long time ago, I believed that *I* was the stronger of the two of us, that it would be *my* role to nurture and support you financially, emotionally—every which way—that I would lead and you would follow, that we would be a partnership, but a partnership in which I was the senior partner. How very wrong and self-deluded I was...'

Across the table from him, Abbie discovered that she was having to swallow past the constricting lump in her throat.

'I didn't want it to be like this,' she heard herself whispering huskily. 'I didn't want to have to leave Cathy with child-minders, to...to...rely on my parents...to have her growing up going without the things that other children had. If I've worked hard, if I've struggled to be commercially successful, it wasn't purely out of ambition for myself... In fact, I didn't want any of it for myself; I wanted it for Cathy... Why are you doing this, Sam?' she demanded. 'Why do you want to undermine me...to make me feel...?'

'To make you feel what, Abbie? What is it I make you feel?'

Abbie had had enough. Standing up, she pushed back her chair, fighting back the tears that threatened to humiliate her as she told him achingly, 'You know how you make me feel. You make me feel that I've failed Cathy...that I've put commercial interest, material gain before her feelings, her needs... Oh, you can say that you admire me, what I've done, but those are only words and I can hear what you're *really* saying, *really* thinking. You're thinking that because of what I've done, because of what I am, I'm somehow less of a woman...less female…less lovable—and, yes, it does hurt. Just as it hurts me knowing that Cathy…my Cathy…'

Abbie couldn't go on, and for the second time in as many weeks she found herself walking out of a restaurant, barely able to control her emotions, whilst all around her the occupants of the other tables were watching with avid but discreet curiosity.

The table where Stuart's sister and her husband had been sitting was empty, she noticed thankfully, so they at least hadn't witnessed her humiliation.

Sam caught up with her just as she reached her car, taking hold of her arm in a firm but oddly gentle grasp, swinging her round to face him, his forehead creased in a small frown as he stated, 'You can't really believe that, Abbie…that I would deliberately try to hurt you…'

'Why not?' she countered, no longer bothering to hide the tears she knew were glittering in her eyes. 'After all, you did before!'

'Oh, Abbie…Abbie…'

Before she could stop him he had wrapped her in his arms as though she were a small child, hugging her, rocking her, smoothing his hand through her hair.

'I never wanted to hurt you,' she heard him whisper emotionally to her. 'Not then…not now… Especially not now.'

'Not now…?' Abbie looked up at him, trying not to think about how good it felt to be close to him like this and how frightening that knowledge was. 'Because…of Cathy?' she asked him painfully.

Out of the corner of her eye she saw a couple walking past them to a car parked a few feet away.

'I've done my best for her,' she told him huskily, part of her shocked at the way she was exposing herself and her vulnerability to him, another part of her in some odd way accepting it as inevitable—as somehow right—causing a conflict of emotion she didn't dare to analyse.

'For God's sake, Abbie…'

The anger she could hear in his voice hurt her. She started to pull away from him, wondering what on earth she was doing, but instead of letting her go he drew her closer to him, the hand still stroking her hair tightening slightly against her scalp as he held her head still and bent his own towards her.

This time there was no pretending to herself that what she was feeling was just an aberration, that what was happening was something outside her control that she didn't really want. She was responding to him, kissing him with a starving hunger she couldn't even try to hide, responding to the fierce, demanding pressure of his mouth in an answer to its question, in a manner as old as time itself…Wanting him, needing him, loving him so intensely that the ache inside her body was an actual physical pain.

'We shouldn't be doing this. I don't… It isn't right,' she tried to whisper to him between frantic kisses, but both his hands were cupping her face now, his mouth biting hungrily at hers as she felt the rapid thud of his heart and the aroused tension of his body.

'Of course it's right,' she heard him whisper back rawly. 'What isn't right is that we should be standing here like a couple of teenagers when… Let me come home with you, Abbie. There's so much we need to say to one another—so much we need to—'

'You mean we still haven't talked about Cathy's wedding?' she asked him dizzily.

She felt dazed, confused almost, by the speed with which things had happened. Her brain told her that she needed time, but her body had more urgent demands and pressed close to Sam's, feeling its every movement, knowing that already he was aroused and that...

'That is one thing we have to discuss,' Sam agreed throatily, 'but not what I had in mind. You do realise, don't you,' he warned her, 'that if we stay here very much longer, if I hold you like this much longer, it isn't going to be a question of whether we make love, but where? And my preference, as you may remember, has always been for a large, comfortable bed and the privacy to explore and enjoy your body, somewhere where—'

'Sam, stop it,' Abbie demanded breathlessly. 'You can't...you mustn't. How can this be happening?' she asked him in bewilderment. 'It isn't... I don't...'

'It's happening because, no matter how much we might try to deny it cerebrally, our bodies, our emotions still need and want each other...'

'No,' Abbie tried to protest, but she knew she was wasting her breath. Right now there was nothing... nothing she wanted more than to feel Sam's naked body above her, around her, within her.

'Abbie, if you don't stop looking at me like that, you know what's going to happen, don't you?' she heard Sam groaning in warning.

'We could...we could go back home...to my house,' she agreed tentatively, aware both of the other couple's interest in them and of her own growing sense of excitement and urgency.

'But,' she added quickly, 'just...just to talk about Cathy and the wedding, that's all.'

'Whatever you want,' Sam agreed, but the look he gave her as he gently helped her into her car said that he knew exactly what it was that she wanted, and that he wanted it as well, and that it had nothing to do with discussing any plans for Cathy's wedding.

It wasn't until she had actually driven home, parked

her car in her drive and seen the lights of Sam's car as he pulled in behind her that the full meaning of what she had invited struck her. But by then it was too late. Sam was getting out of his car, and as she followed suit and stood waiting for him her body was seized by a flood of weakening emotions that made it impossible for her to move. Fatalistically, she watched him walk towards her, knowing that it was too late now to stop what had been set in motion.

As Sam reached her he touched her face gently and then took her house keys from her nerveless fingers, holding her cold hand in the oddly reassuring warmth of his as he unlocked the door and then, almost tenderly, urged her inside.

Just inside the kitchen she paused, her voice husky and hesitant as she pleaded, 'We don't really need to talk about…about the wedding now, do we? After all, Cathy and Stuart haven't even set a proper formal date yet.'

'Second thoughts?' Sam asked her softly.

Abbie couldn't pretend not to know what he meant.

'That was…that was the whole purpose of our meeting,' she reminded him shakily.

'It *was*, I agree,' Sam replied semi-cryptically. 'But…'

'But what?' Abbie demanded, reminding herself that she was an adult and that attack was supposed to be the best means of defence. She was no longer a woman who could allow herself to take a passive role in a relationship, or in life itself.

'Do you really need to ask?' Sam derided her gently. 'Didn't what happened between us earlier make it obvious?'

'Nothing happened,' Abbie denied hastily, hurriedly finding some measure of release from the tension gripping her by going to fill the kettle, an automatic action which common sense warned her was not a logical or wise thing to do when she was desperately regretting allowing Sam to come back with her and wishing that he would leave.

'Oh, no? Tell that to my body,' Sam drawled self-mockingly, and then made her heart stand still and panic explode inside her as he added devastatingly, 'And your own. After all,' he went on quietly, 'whatever else went wrong between us, whatever other mistakes I might have made, sexually, things were...

'Do you have any idea what it felt like?' he demanded, the harshness in his voice shocking her. 'To sleep alone in the same bed where only hours before you had lain there with me, making those soft, keening sounds of pleasure you always made when we made love, making those delicious, satisfied little gasps that meant that you wanted me. Have you any idea of what it felt like, waking up in an empty, cold bed without you beside me...reaching out for you and not finding you there? Did you know that in the night, in your sleep, you used to snuggle up next to me, curling your body just as tightly as you could into mine, as though you couldn't bear to break the contact with me? I used to lie there watching you, enjoying the pleasure of knowing how completely mine you were and how much I loved you.'

Something in the way he was looking at her, in the dark sombreness of his eyes which matched the starkly melancholic tone of his voice, filled Abbie with a mixture of achingly painful emotions. His words brought back feelings she had kept hidden. Not just from others, but from herself as well. Because she hadn't been able to bear to acknowledge that she felt them. Instead she had focused and held onto her anger, needing it to sustain her, to cling to, because if she hadn't...if she had allowed herself to acknowledge those other feelings, those other pains, she just wouldn't have been able to survive.

And now Sam was forcing her to remember them, forcing her to acknowledge a pain so intense and so overpowering that she instinctively fought to withdraw from it and deny it, panic flooding through her as she turned to face him like an animal at bay, crying out bitterly, 'No, you did not love me. If you had you would never have doubted me, never have believed that I'd been unfaithful to you. You talk about how *you* felt. What do you imagine your rejection…your accusations did to me? You didn't love me. You couldn't have done. You…'

'Abbie, you're wrong. I did…'

She had said the wrong thing, done the wrong thing, Abbie recognised as Sam crossed the distance between them, taking hold of her upper arms as he spoke urgently to her.

'No. No, you didn't,' she denied. 'You couldn't have done…'

She knew he must have heard the panic in her voice, and her whole body started to tremble as he demanded, 'Why do you say that? Why is it so important to you to believe that I didn't love you? I freely acknowledge that the worst, the biggest mistake I've ever made in my life was to deny my own child, but the last thing I'm going to do now is to compound that betrayal by lying about the feelings, the love I had for you.'

'It wasn't love…it was just sex,' Abbie insisted frantically.

'Just sex… For you, maybe,' Sam told her quietly. 'But not for me…never for me. Was that it? Was that why you were able to walk away from me so easily,

Abbie—because it was only sex so far as *you* were concerned?' he asked her bitterly.

To walk away from him so easily. Abbie just managed to catch back a sob of mingled anguish and hysteria. If only he knew… If only he knew just what she had suffered…just how much damage had been done—how hard it had been for her to go on without him. The only thing, the only person who had kept her going had been Cathy…the knowledge that she had to be strong, that she had to survive for Cathy's sake. And even then…

She shivered, remembering the stern warning the doctor had given her that if she didn't start eating properly and looking after herself better she was in real danger of losing her baby. That had been in the early weeks after the break-up, when the very thought of food, never mind the sight and taste of it, had made her feel acutely nauseous. When all she had seemed to do was to cry and mourn the loss of her love, and when all she had wanted was to escape from the too heavy burden of her heartache and misery… And this was what Sam called easy…

Easy. Even now, after all these years, the muffled echoes of her old pain still rumbled threateningly in the distance, making her want to cower and shiver, to hide herself from the devastating effect of that threat like a small child cowering in terror from the first warning rumble of thunder. But she wasn't going to let him see that—no, not for a minute. Her pride wouldn't allow her to. Tilting her chin, she made herself look at him with forced calm.

'I suppose it must have been. After all, at that age it's hard to tell the difference, isn't it? And I was after all particularly inexperienced and naive,' she added disparagingly. 'Sex and love, so far as I was concerned then, were the same thing…'

'But now, of course, you do know the difference. Is that it?' Sam challenged her grimly.

As she heard the suppressed anger in his voice Abbie looked up at him, her heart jolting heavily against her ribs at the look in his eyes. Somehow, somewhere, she had made a misjudgement, and a bad one, she recognised. But it was too late now to regret or recall what she had already said. She could only go on, or give in, and she certainly wasn't going to do that.

'Yes, I suppose I do,' she agreed coolly, her voice only giving the smallest betraying tremble as she tried to pull herself free of his grip. 'It would be a rather odd thing if I hadn't, don't you think?' she added for good measure. The last thing she wanted to let him guess was that there hadn't been any man in her life since him, that when she woke up in the night, her body aching, her bed empty...

'Good, then you'll know exactly what this is, then, won't you?' she heard Sam saying to her as, instead of releasing her as she expected, he tightened his hold on her, drawing her back against his body, lowering his head towards her own.

Desperately Abbie tried to turn her face to one side, to avoid and escape what she knew was going to happen, but Sam anticipated her, releasing her arm and holding the side of her head and face instead, his palm against her jaw, his fingertips in her hair as he held her still.

The feel of his warm breath against her face made the whole of her body tremble in self-betrayal, her vocal denial of what she knew was going to happen a small, explosive sound that held more panic than any real insistence, Abbie recognised.

'Which does your experience tell you that this is, Abbie?' Sam demanded savagely against her mouth.

'I know exactly what it is,' she threw equally fiercely back at him. 'But you can't—'

'If you know, then I don't have to make any excuses for myself, do I?' Sam interrupted her thickly. 'And, since I can't deceive you, there isn't any point in any pretence between us, is there…?'

Abbie tried to tell him that so far as she was concerned there wasn't any point, any reason for there to be anything between them any more, but as soon as she opened her mouth Sam covered it with his own.

A shocking feeling of pleasure and familiarity swamped her, and Abbie felt her body respond to the demanding pressure of his mouth.

This was no tentative wooing kiss such as a new lover might give; this was the kiss of a man who felt he had no need for any preliminary skirmishes—the kind of kiss that was permissible, acceptable, only between established and very passionate lovers, Abbie acknowledged dizzily as she tried to withdraw from the sensual intimacy of Sam's kiss and discovered, with heart-numbing pain, that not only was *he* preventing her from doing so but her own body was also aiding and abetting him.

How could her lips be clinging so wantonly to his? How could they be opening, softening, her tongue shyly meeting the much more rhythmic and far deeper thrusts of his? How could her body be quivering, melting, yielding so obviously and so easily beneath the silent demands of his kiss?

His kiss… It wasn't just a kiss he was imposing on her wretchedly vulnerable and traitorous senses, it was…it was…a seduction…a passion…a possession of breathtaking magnitude and barefaced daring, Abbie acknowledged shakily as Sam drew her even closer to his body. His hands slid down over her back, shaping the curve of her waist, her hips, cupping the soft roundness of her buttocks as he…

Beneath his mouth she gave a small moan of protest, her whole body shuddering in shocked reaction as he responded to its awareness of him with an even deeper and more explicitly sensual thrusting of his tongue, matched by the increasingly urgent movement of his hips—his groin against the vulnerable softness of her own body.

She was literally trembling helplessly from head to foot, Abbie recognised, totally incapable of controlling or concealing her physical reaction to him. And that was just the outer sign of her physical awareness of him… just the tip of the physical iceberg he had aroused within her—if iceberg was the correct term to describe a feeling that was generating so much heat.

How long was it since her body had experienced that instantly and dismayingly familiar throbbing ache? That wanton driving urge to press herself even closer to him, to match the movement of his body with some equally sensually explicit movements of her own, to…to reach out and touch him, to press her lips against his skin, to the damp hollow at the base of his throat where the tiny beads of sexually generated sweat collected, to stroke her fingertips through the soft darkness of the body hair that darkened his chest, and all the while to feel her own excitement and urgency increasing in time to match his whilst she teased him…

While she teased both of them with little, little strokes and licks, watching the increasingly open throb of the pulse at the base of his throat, knowing that its urgency was matched, more than matched, by the equally powerful and far, far more openly erotic pulsing of another part of his body, knowing that when she finally lowered her head and teased that place…that part…with the tip of her tongue, in the same way that she was his throat, he would be completely unable to hold back his moan of anguished pleasure in what she was doing.

Inwardly, secretly, her own desire would be fed and multiplied by the sense of power in her womanhood that it gave her to know how much she could arouse him, how close to the edge of his self-control she could drive him, how intense the degree of pleasure she could give him just by the delicate brush of her lips and tongue...

How long? Too long...too long...

Abbie heard herself moaning helplessly in need, her body held in thrall to the powerful pull of her dangerous memories, overriding the protective mechanism of her brain as it struggled to stop what was happening to her. Instinctively she moved closer to Sam, her hips mirroring the movement of his, her hands sliding up over his shoulders and then down over his back, feeling the hard-packed muscles, still surely as strong and taut as they had ever been, his waist just as narrow, his buttocks...

Abbie could feel the heat engulfing her as her hands, her fingers, ignoring the shocked recoil of her brain, dug into the deliciously hard muscles, kneading with familiar erotic intimacy. What was it about that part of a man's anatomy that made it such a pleasure to touch and hold onto?

The same instinct that made a man seek out the soft warmth of a woman's breasts? Abbie wondered in dazed, sensual bemusement as Sam, almost as though he had read and then acted upon her own thoughts, cupped hers in his hands, caressing them gently at first and then, as her mouth opened eagerly beneath his in uncontrollable and uninhibited pleasure at the way he was touching her, more urgently, more possessively. Abbie started as she felt her nipples stiffen in overjoyed response to his touch.

How was it that her body was so immediately, so overwhelmingly responsive to his touch? Especially when, in all the years they had been apart, she had been so sure, so convinced that when he had destroyed their love he had destroyed her desire for him, her ability to respond to him as well. After all, how could she be physically aroused by a man she didn't love...couldn't love? How could *he* still want a woman he believed had deceived him...a woman he couldn't trust?

How could either of them now be here like this— together—their bodies as urgent and hot for one another as they had been all those years ago? Wanting the other with all the impatient, hot-blooded eagerness and desire she remembered and had tried so hard to forget. But now, added to that youthful eagerness, there was a sharp-edged hunger...a knowledge that came from maturity and a full awareness of themselves and their sexuality.

The shy young teenager who had so gladly allowed Sam to help her to explore and get to know her own sexuality had been replaced by a woman of equal sexual potency, Abbie recognised, an active and not a passive partner in love's sensual dance. A woman whose desire was suddenly so strong and all-consuming that she herself was taken totally off guard by its demanding power.

She could feel Sam starting to release her mouth, his tongue withdrawing from its intimacy with her, and immediately she made a low sound of protest deep in her throat, closing her lips around it and sucking sensually on it, her teeth biting passionately at his bottom lip as she felt the violent surge of response jolt through his body.

'Abbie...Abbie...'

Had his voice really held such a deep, almost guttural note of male arousal and awareness of her female power all those years before? Abbie rather thought not. Then *he* had always been the one in control, even if it had been a loving, careful, protective type of control. Now, she suspected, without knowing how she had come to any such knowledge, he was nowhere near so much the master of the situation. She could feel his hands trembling against her breasts, and when his thumb-tips caressed her hard nipples his body reacted just as intensely to that stimulation as her own.

She could feel his breathing quicken and his heart start to race as she teased his mouth with hot, biting kisses, tasting not just the musky male heat of his mouth but the euphoria of her own power to command his sexuality and arousal as well.

'Oh, God, have you any idea what you're doing to me? How much I've wanted this...ached for it... hungered for it...for you?' Abbie heard him demanding as her mouth teased its way along his throat and down over his jaw. Her heart started to thump heavily in recognition of the excitement she had felt earlier. Remembering just what her then almost shy kisses at the base of his throat had been a prelude to.

Would *he* remember? Would he? And if he did how would he react? Or would he...?

Her heart leapt in a mixture of excitement and nervous uncertainty as her lips touched first the damp of his Adam's apple and then slid moistly downwards. She could feel the heat suddenly burn up under Sam's skin, the sweat beading his throat as he started to shudder so deeply and violently that for a second it actually alarmed her.

But when she made to withdraw from him his hands clamped round her arms, holding her against his body as he begged, through gritted teeth, 'Oh, God, Abbie, don't stop now, for God's sake. Don't stop now... If you only knew...'

The rest of what he was trying to say was lost as his body became convulsed by a second series of shudders against her, and her own desire and arousal rose up to meet his own, her tongue-tip lapping eagerly at the moistness of his skin, her mind automatically registering the words he was saying to her and reacting to them as he demanded urgently, 'Touch me, Abbie... Undress me...my shirt...yes...that's it...unfasten it...'

She was trembling so much that in the end she had to use both hands, wrenching the buttons free rather than easing them through the small holes, but Sam seemed unaware of her clumsiness, or of any damage she might have inflicted on his shirt, his chest expanding rapidly as he drew in a deep breath of air and then raised his hands to slide his fingers into her hair and urge her towards his body. She could feel his spine arching, his body taut as she kissed the hot male flesh she had exposed.

His skin was tanned darker than she remembered, but the texture of it, the feel and the smell—especially the smell—was exactly the same. She could feel wetness against her face as she leaned her head against his chest and felt the familiar prickle of his body hair tickling her skin. But it was several seconds before she recognised that it was caused by her own tears.

Tears...from her...for what?

Bewildered and confused, she lifted her hand to her face, but Sam forestalled her, his fingers gentle, tender almost, as he touched her damp face and then lifted his fingers to his mouth, tasting her tears, his eyes darkening as he said roughly, 'Oh, God, Abbie. What have we done to each other, to ourselves? Why have we...?'

Abbie could feel herself starting to tremble. She didn't want to talk about what had happened. She didn't want to resurrect the past and risk destroying what they were sharing now. She didn't want to have to analyse and dissect what had happened…to bring to life the pain she had always made herself deny she had ever felt. She was too afraid that if she did…once she did…

Quickly she turned her head and started to kiss Sam's chest. Fiercely, almost angrily at first, and then more lingeringly, savouring its taste and texture as her heightened emotions relayed the familiar flavour and scent of him to her. One small, hard male nipple was temptingly close to her lips. She moved her head slightly and let them close gently over it, savouring the texture of it, turning her tongue slowly and then more boldly over it.

She could feel Sam's body tense and then tremble. Somehow or other one of her hands had slid down his chest and was resting just above his belt. She could feel him draw in his breath as she slowly and deliberately started to circle his nipple with the tip of her tongue. She waited until he had started to relax slightly and expel his breath and then she closed her mouth around him and very, very slowly started to suck.

The sound that rattled in his throat seemed to have been dragged from the very depths of his body. His arms closed so tightly around her that she felt he might almost crush the breath out of her lungs.

'If you don't stop that right now, I'm going…' she heard him protest thickly, his voice dying away as she deliberately increased the delicately sensual pressure of her mouth, her own excitement and arousal kicking into a higher gear as she acknowledged the pleasure it gave her to know how dangerously close to the edge of his self-control she was pushing him. If she could arouse him so much just by doing this, how would he feel…what would he do…what might happen if she touched him more intimately? Teased just a little bit more provocatively…? If she…?

'There's only one way to make you see what you're doing to me and that's to give you a taste of your own medicine,' she heard Sam telling her, his voice unexpectedly taking on a much firmer note as he caught her completely off guard by swinging her up into his arms and holding her there as he headed for the kitchen door.

One hand was holding her imprisoned whilst she clung onto him, half afraid that he might drop her, and the other... The other, she realised with a small start of excited nervousness, was reaching for the fastening of her bra...

'Where are you going? What are you doing?' she demanded breathlessly, her protest drowned out by her small gasp of surprise not so much at the ease, rather more at the delicious feeling of pleasure it gave her to know that the only thing that now lay between the feel of his hands...his mouth on her body...was the thin silkiness of her top.

'I'm taking you to bed, where I can show you exactly what it feels like to have someone tormenting you, playing with you the way you were just doing with me, and what the consequences of such dangerous behaviour are,' Sam told her, mock seriously, adding smoothly, 'Unless, of course, you'd rather stay down here? That kitchen table looks just about the right height—although perhaps at your age your back can't take—'

'There is absolutely nothing wrong with me—neither my age nor my back,' Abbie interrupted him hotly. 'I am, after all, still six years younger than you are, Sam, and it's pretty obvious that you're hardly incapable or past it...'

'I'm delighted to hear that you think so,' Sam told her, laughing at her and adding wickedly, 'But shouldn't you perhaps reserve such unstinting praise until it's actually deserved? And I do intend to deserve it,' he added slowly, and this time there was no laughter in his eyes nor his voice, Abbie noticed as her heart gave a terrifying and unnerving bump and her nipples, to her consternation and embarrassment, suddenly peaked so hard that they were clearly discernible beneath her top.

Sam had seen them, she knew, and the sight of him focusing his attention on them visually, whilst his mouth opened and his tongue-tip touched his upper lip, aroused a feeling inside her body that made her shockingly and shamefully aware of just how little it would take now for him to bring her to complete physical fulfilment.

The first time she had reached orgasm had been an earth-shattering and unfamiliar experience for her, the pinnacle of a slow, tender journey. To have to acknowledge now that merely the thought of him touching her, suckling on her sensitively aroused nipples, was virtually enough to cause her to reach that same pinnacle was intensely disturbing.

'Don't move, Abbie,' she heard Sam warn her thickly, 'because if you do there's no way we're going to make it through that door, never mind as far as your bed.'

At first she thought he had actually read her mind and knew what she was feeling, but as she gazed in shaken bemusement into his face she realised that it was his own arousal he was referring to.

'This can't be happening,' she heard her protesting as he carried her upstairs. 'We aren't a couple of teenagers. We don't even…'

'We don't what?' Sam demanded gruffly as he walked through the open bedroom door and gently slid her to her feet, standing with her body to his body so that she could feel each and every inch of him against her. 'We don't have a right to feel desire? To want each other…? Who says so? Not our bodies, Abbie. Not our senses…not our emotions… They all say… They *all* say…' he repeated, and his voice slowed and thickened as he reached out and held her face.

He kissed her slowly and gently at first, and then more urgently, as though he just couldn't help himself, as though he had starved for her, hungered for her, as though she was the only woman he had ever wanted…as though he knew that *he* was the only man she had ever wanted.

'Oh, God, Abbie,' she heard him whisper in muffled anguish as his mouth slid down over her body, leaving a damp trail on the fabric of her top before finally closing over her breast, drawing hungrily on her nipple, suckling on it, rolling his tongue around it, nibbling it gently and oh, so mind-destroyingly erotically with his teeth, so that Abbie wanted to rip her top off herself and hold him against her.

She couldn't remember them getting undressed, only the sweetly savage pleasure of their shared nakedness, of her own recognition that all that had changed about his body was that it was even more potently male than ever, and all that had changed about her own was that it was even more keenly responsive to him.

She tensed briefly once, hesitant, trembling with a mixture of uncertainty and unbearable longing as Sam knelt in front of her, gently removing her briefs, first planting kisses in an erotic circle around her navel and then moving lower, so that she was trembling violently with arousal and emotion by the time he buried his face against her naked body, breathing in the scent of her, openly delighting in the warm, damp feel of her body hair against his skin.

'No,' Abbie protested, trying quickly to withdraw from him as his lips brushed the delicate flesh of her groin. If he touched her now he would find her so wet, so ready for him…and if he didn't…

The small moan she gave must have alerted him to what was happening to her. Must, she recognised in hot dismay, have reactivated some old memory of the signs and sounds of her arousal, because his hand immediately gently covered her sex, almost as though he was trying to comfort and steady her, and then he was lifting her onto the bed and following her down onto it, unashamedly displaying his own arousal...

What was it about the sight of that one special man's arousal that could literally make a woman feel weak at the knees? Fill her with a mixture of awe and protective awareness at the unexpected beauty of something that was both so proudly male and almost ridiculously vulnerable, so strong and yet so potentially weak, so dangerously easy for the right woman to arouse and excite, and even more dangerously easy for her to destroy and deflate. The wrong word, the wrong action...even just the wrong look.

'What is it you want, Abbie?' she heard Sam asking her huskily. 'My hand...my mouth...my body...'

'You. I want you,' Abbie heard herself moaning back in frantic response, and her own thoughts were forgotten, overtaken by the relief of Sam touching her, lowering himself against her so that she could feel him, so that she could open her legs and wrap herself around him, silently urging him to move closer, closer, deeper and yet even deeper, until she was matching the shockingly easily remembered rhythm of his thrusts, moving with them and against them, their voices rising and mingling as they cried out to each other in mutual need and arousal, mutual exultation and ecstasy, as their bodies exploded into almost immediate orgasm. And then low-murmured whispers of mutual exhaustion as the words of praise and pleasure were whispered in each other's ears...

*   *   *

Abbie opened her eyes in sleepy confusion. Sam wasn't sleeping on his normal side of the bed. Her body was all tangled up with his and her hair was trapped underneath his arm.

Sam... Abbie came abruptly wide awake. This wasn't then, some twenty years ago. This was now... Now— and she had done the unforgivable and unbelievable. And, what was more, she hadn't just stopped at doing it once. To her chagrin she recognised that she must have eventually fallen asleep in Sam's arms, her body so sated and exhausted by the pleasure he had given her that she hadn't even had time to move away from him, because she was still lying where she had been the last time they had made love, in that easy, comfortable, gentle spoon position they had discovered in the early months of their marriage...

Sam must have reached out for the duvet they had kicked to one side earlier, when their lovemaking had been anything but gentle or easy, because it was lying over and around them both, and in the dim light she could see the way their clothes were scattered all over the bedroom floor... She made a move to pull away from him, but in his sleep Sam tightened his hold on her.

She really ought to wake him up, to tell him... She really ought... She gave a small yawn and then another deeper one; the temptation to snuggle back down again next to him was too overpowering to be ignored. After all, what harm could it do now? In the morning they could discuss what had happened, acknowledge that it had been a mistake...something best forgotten, ignored... A physical reaction between them that neither of them had really been able to control and which, she suspected, had caught them both off guard.

Indulging in a night of passionate sex with her ex-husband might not be the most sensible thing she had

ever done in her life, Abbie acknowledged, but there had
been extenuating circumstances and she knew it was
something she would never do again. She was allowed
to make some mistakes, wasn't she? she demanded
bravely of her nagging conscience.

He doesn't love you, she reminded herself. You don't
love him. Maybe, she admitted, but they had loved one
another once, and tonight...

Tonight what? Tonight she had succumbed to a need,
a desire, a yearning she had not even really known she
had had?

It was too late to regret what had happened now, she
told herself tiredly. All she could do was a damage-
limitation exercise and that included not getting herself
into a panic right now over something she couldn't really
do anything about until Sam woke up and they could
discuss the whole situation rationally—not something
that was likely to happen if she insisted on waking him
now, when he was so obviously very deeply asleep.

Tomorrow, she suspected, he would be as eager
to dismiss what had happened as she was herself.
Tomorrow... She gave another final yawn and closed her
eyes, her body relaxing back into sleep.

At her side Sam opened his eyes and looked down
into her face, his own expression sombre. Had he done
the right thing or had he well and truly blown everything?

When she looked at him in the morning would it be
with hate or—dared he let himself begin to hope the
impossible?

Gently, very gently, he pulled her sleeping body
closer to his own, taking her intimately close to his side
and holding her there.

CHAPTER SEVEN

'MUM...Mum, what's Dad's car doing outside? Why...? Oh!'

Abbie sat bolt upright in bed, frantically clutching the duvet to her naked body, her face burning with a scarlet tide of guilt and embarrassment as Cathy burst into the bedroom and came to a stunned halt, her mouth rounding in a startled 'O' of shock as she stared at the two occupants of her mother's bed.

'Oh,' she repeated, but this time her face was wreathed in smiles of intense, mischievous joy as she looked from Abbie's flushed, embarrassed face to Sam's far more impassively contained and controlled one.

'Oh, this is wonderful, marvellous...just wait until I tell Stuart what's happened. Oh, I'm so thrilled. *When* did it happen? *When* did you two decide to get back together again? And fancy not saying anything...how *could* you keep it a secret? Oh, this is wonderful...wonderful. Oh, Mum, I'm so thrilled...'

Happy tears had filled Cathy's eyes and they splashed down her cheeks as she ran towards the bed and hugged them both, Abbie first and then Sam, before turning round and rushing back to the door, calling over her shoulder as she hurried through it, 'Stuart's waiting downstairs. I made him drop me off because I was so worried about you, Mum, you seemed so down. If only I'd really known what was going on. Just wait until I tell him about this... Just wait until I tell everyone...'

'Cathy,' Abbie protested, having at last managed to control her shock enough to find her voice, but it was too late; she could already hear Cathy excitedly telling Stuart what had happened—or rather what she believed had happened.

'Stuart's as thrilled as I am,' she announced, re-appearing in the doorway moments later. 'We won't stay; it was just a quick call. Not, I'm sure, that either of you two will mind,' she added mischievously, with an arch look from her parents to the clothes that still lay scattered so betrayingly on the bedroom floor. 'Have fun,' she added with a grin. 'And remember,' she added mock warningly, 'always make sure you have safe sex.'

Safe sex. Abbie could hear Cathy laughing as she ran back downstairs. At her side she heard Sam clearing his throat and then apologising huskily.

'I'm sorry…that was something I should have thought about last night, but…well, it's not really been an issue for me for so long that—'

'That what?' Abbie challenged him bitterly, but keeping her voice low so that Cathy couldn't hear them. 'That you felt that it was all right to assume that I would have taken all the necessary precautions?'

She could feel reaction to what had happened setting in. A sense of angry helplessness and rage filled her as she contemplated the full consequences of everything that had occurred.

'Well, unfortunately that wasn't the case. Despite what you seem to think, and quite obviously unlike yours, my life does not include the kind of… intimacy…the kind of sex life that makes it necessary,' she concluded stiffly.

She wasn't quite sure why his obvious belief that she would automatically be using some kind of protective birth control should hurt her so much, but she knew that it did.

'Besides,' she added fiercely, allowing her voice to

rise slightly as she heard the back door open and then close again and the sound of a car engine firing as Cathy and Stuart left, 'as far as I'm concerned, we've got far more important things to worry about than the unlikely chance—the *extremely* unlikely chance—of my conceiving your child for a second time.'

For the first time since Cathy had burst into the bedroom, Abbie managed to look directly at Sam. Like her, he had sat up in bed immediately Cathy had rushed in, but unlike her he had made no move to cover his naked body with the duvet—no cowering beneath its inadequate protection with a guilty expression on *his* face.

In the clear morning his torso looked just as firmly fleshed and muscled as it had felt last night. There was a small bruise at the base of his throat, Abbie recognised, feeling the heat burn up over her body as she remembered how it had got there, and his mouth had that slightly swollen look that came from being passionately and very intensely kissed...like her own. She touched her lips tentatively with her tongue-tip and her face burned an even deeper shade of pink.

'What's wrong?' Sam asked her, frowning. 'Sore?'

Sore? Abbie stared at him, her colour rising despite her attempt to check it.

'What's wrong?' she repeated. 'Do you really need to ask? *You* heard Cathy... I should think the whole town has probably heard her by now. She thinks that you and I...that we're—'

'Giving our relationship a second chance?' Sam supplied for her.

He sounded amazingly unconcerned, Abbie acknowledged, his lack of reaction somehow increasing her own sense of panic and anger.

'You heard her,' she repeated. 'She's already told Stuart...and right now no doubt she's on her way to tell everyone else. Why didn't you say something to her...stop her...?'

'Why didn't you?' Sam countered.

Abbie stared at him.

'Like what?' she demanded. 'Like just because she'd found us in bed together it didn't mean...it *doesn't* mean... You know what I'm trying to say,' Abbie accused him, looking away from him.

It irritated her that she should feel at such a disadvantage with him, that *she* should be the one clinging protectively and defensively to what, after all, was her own duvet, whilst he lay there lounging back against the pillows for all the world as though it were a perfectly normal event for them to have spent the night together and then been discovered in bed together by their daughter.

As she shrugged petulantly the duvet slipped down even further, revealing the taut flatness of his stomach. There was another small, betraying bruise right next to his navel, Abbie recognised, unable to tear her gaze away from the small purple mark. How many others were there? she wondered uncomfortably, her face flushing as she wriggled uneasily, unable to accept the physical evidence of her own passion and desire.

'What is it?' she heard Sam asking her, and then, as he looked from her flushed, averted face and glanced down at his body, she could hear the amusement in his voice as he murmured, 'Ah, yes, no communal sports club showers for me for the next few days, hmm? Especially when you think where the others are...'

'What others?' Abbie demanded, her head whipping round as she stared angrily at him. 'Where—'

'Don't tell me you've forgotten already,' Sam teased her. 'But of course if you *really* want me to refresh your memory...'

He made to throw back the duvet completely, but

Abbie stopped him, her face burning a hot, embarrassed red as she remembered exactly where it was that she had bitten so deliberately into the seductive smoothness of his male flesh, and the little trail of tell-tale marks she had no doubt left along the insides of his thighs.

'What are we going to do, Sam?' she demanded helplessly, unable to conceal her anxiety and vulnerability any longer. 'Cathy thinks that we've been reconciled... that...that we're making plans to get back together. That's what she's going to tell everyone and we both know that it just isn't true, that what happened was just...just...'

'Just what,' Sam challenged her, his voice suddenly unexpectedly hard, as though he was trying to warn her about something. About reading the wrong meaning into what had happened between them. About assuming that because they had made love, had sex, it meant something more...meant that he still had feelings for her, still cared for her.

Did he *really* think that she was idiotic enough to delude herself that, because he had been sexually aroused, it meant that he must also have been emotionally aroused? Hadn't she *already* learned the hardest way possible that love was an emotion that just could not exist between them?

'Just sex,' Abbie responded lightly, proud of the way her voice didn't tremble or quiver, betraying what she was really feeling.

'Just sex,' Sam repeated harshly. 'I see. Tell me something, Abbie, how many other men have there been with whom you have had "just sex" since you and I—'

'You have no right to ask me that sort of question,' Abbie interrupted him furiously. 'No right at all. How would you like it if I did the same thing to you? You wouldn't, would you?' she told him, answering her own question.

'You surprise me, Abbie, do you know that?' Sam told her heavily. 'Hypocrisy is the very last thing I would ever have expected from you.'

Hypocrisy? Abbie tensed. What was he trying to imply? That he had guessed that she was lying to him when she claimed that last night had been 'just sex', that he knew that for her…? She took a deep breath, her heart beating fast as she was brought face to face with a truth she had been fighting to avoid ever since it had first confronted her last night.

She was not *still* in love with Sam, she denied fiercely. How could she be? After what he had done…after what he had said. What had happened last night had just been a…fluke. A cruel prank on the part of fate. It meant nothing—nothing at all…nothing.

'You were quite happy to go to bed with me, to have sex with me,' she heard Sam saying bitterly, 'just so long as it could be kept secret…just so long as no one else knew—more than happy, in fact, as I recall last night's events. But when it comes to anyone else knowing what happened between us…'

'Yes, all right, maybe I am a hypocrite,' Abbie agreed, too relieved that he hadn't guessed what she was really feeling to deny his allegation. 'How would you feel in my shoes? Would you want everyone knowing what you had done? Can you imagine what it's going to be like for me living here now? It's all right for you. You can walk away from it all, go back to your real life, walk away from me—just like you did before.'

It hurt unbearably after what they had shared last night that they should now be fighting like this.

'Oh, God, why did Cathy have to come and find us? Why? I'll *have* to tell her the truth, and—'

'Do you really think that's a good idea?' Sam interrupted her quietly.

'What else can I do?' Abbie challenged him. 'She's got to know the truth sooner or later. I just wish that I could have stopped her before she'd broadcast her story to half the town. I can just imagine what Stuart's parents are going to say when they find out about this—especially his mother. She already thinks I'm a total failure as a mother...especially as the mother of her precious son's prospective wife.

'It isn't for my own sake I'm concerned. It's Cathy I'm bothered about. I *hate* the thought of Stuart's mother criticising her, finding fault with her, blaming her for what she considers to be *my* failures. At the moment Cathy is far too much in love to realise the problems she might have to face with Stuart's mother, and I hate knowing that I'm probably making them even worse for her.'

'If Cathy feels anything other than love and immense pride for you and all that you've done for her, then she's not the girl I know she is,' Sam told her firmly. 'But as for Stuart's mother—have you thought that perhaps in the circumstances it might be better to leave matters as they stand?'

'What matters?' Abbie asked him suspiciously.

'Since Cathy already believes that we are attempting to re-establish our relationship, perhaps it's better to allow her—and everyone else—to continue to believe that,' Sam explained. 'At least for the time being. It will, I suspect, be far easier to simply let our new "relationship" flounder and then fail than to force Cathy to accept a truth she quite plainly doesn't want to see. Easier for her, easier for everyone else and easier for us as well.'

'You'd do that? Pretend that we...that last night...that we're planning to get back together again? Make that kind of sacrifice for Cathy's sake? Why?' she demanded in disbelief. 'When…'

'Perhaps I feel I owe her one or two sacrifices,' Sam told her sombrely. 'And besides—'

'No, don't say any more. Whatever it is, I don't want to hear it,' Abbie interrupted him fiercely.

Had he any idea how much what he had just said— what his words had just revealed—shook her emotionally? How much it hurt her knowing that he was prepared to make sacrifices for Cathy's sake, knowing that he wanted to protect Cathy from the potentially unpleasant fall-out of malicious gossip about what had happened, whilst at the same time he made absolutely no acknowledgement of the fact that *she* too might be in need of some protection from those same wagging tongues? But then *she*, of course, did not matter. She had *never* mattered. How could she have done when all she was to him was someone who aroused his most basic sensual male drive, someone who aroused him physically but who failed to touch his emotions?

'Abbie.'

She froze as she felt him touch her lightly on her arm, wrenching herself away from him, unaware of the pain in his eyes as he saw the way she was withdrawing from him—a sure sign, if he needed one, that she was already regretting what had happened last night. Unlike him. He…

'I'm sorry if I've upset you,' he began quietly.

But Abbie wouldn't let him continue, her eyes bright with emotion as she turned back to him and told him sharply, 'You have not upset me, Sam.' She added for good measure, '*You* could not upset me. *You* don't have that power. Not any longer. For someone to hurt *me* emotionally I have to care about *them* emotionally.'

'Abbie,' Sam began again, but Abbie shook her head.

'We could never convince people that we're thinking of getting back together again,' she continued starkly. 'No one would ever believe it.'

'Cathy already does,' Sam pointed out dryly. 'And so far as I can see it certainly seems the most practical solution to our present situation—the only really viable solution, in fact,' he added, before Abbie could deny what he was saying.

'You really mean it, don't you?' Abbie asked him in disbelief. 'Cathy would be flattered if she knew the lengths you're prepared to go to to protect her and make her happy—'

'Cathy must never know,' Sam interrupted her curtly.

'Never? Just how long do you envisage us playing out this ridiculous charade?' Abbie challenged him, adding, 'It will never work.'

'It will if we want it to, and besides, it won't be for that long. Only until Cathy is married,' Sam argued.

'What?' Abbie was appalled. 'But they're not planning to marry until next year. 'You can't—we can't... Oh, no, Sam...' she protested. 'That's impossible.'

'Nothing is ever impossible,' Sam corrected her. 'Difficult, impractical, hazardous and foolhardy, maybe, but impossible—no.'

Against her will, hearing the wry note in his voice and seeing the glint of humour in his eyes as she listened to him, Abbie felt her own sense of humour bubbling up in response, soothing away her tension and anger. A small responsive smile curled her mouth in rueful acknowledgement of what he was saying, much as she struggled to suppress it, to remind herself that this was a man who in the past had hurt her very badly, and that her own fear of that hurt was not confined just to the past.

Last night in Sam's arms she had forgotten how much

he had hurt her and remembered only the intense pleasure of their shared sensual need for one another. But she was too mature, too wise now, surely, to deceive herself that last night had been love.

'We can't do it, Sam,' she protested, and then added quietly, '*I* can't…it's too difficult.'

'Would it be any easier telling Cathy the truth?' Sam challenged her.

Abbie looked at him and swallowed hard, knowing when she was beaten, shaking her head as she admitted reluctantly, 'No. But I can't just lie to everyone and pretend—lie about a relationship between us that just does not and could not exist,' she added, her revulsion and distress evident in her voice. 'This is my home,' she reminded him. 'And it's my family, my friends, my…business contacts you're talking about deceiving. As I said, it's all right for you—you can just walk away and—'

'And what? Be branded the bad guy for the second time round?' Sam suggested grimly. 'Oh, yes, I know perfectly well exactly what everyone here thinks of me. The man who was so possessively jealous of his wife, so afraid of losing her that he prompted the very thing he most feared by his own idiotic behaviour. All right,' he told Abbie angrily, 'so *you* can't lie. So what exactly do you suggest that we do? Tell the truth, whatever that might be?'

Abbie felt unable to answer him.

'Well, come on, then—or have you got some other solution, some other alternative? Look, Abbie,' Sam told her more gently, 'you can see how much it meant to Cathy to believe that the two of us were getting back together again. Why spoil things for her and create a hell of a lot of problems for ourselves by forcing her to accept a truth she just doesn't want to know? Why not let her have the reassurance of believing what she wants to believe? She wants to believe that you and I are rebuilding our relationship—why disillusion her? After all, these months leading up to her marriage are going to be difficult enough for her anyway—I remember how tense and on edge you were, and you didn't have Stuart's mother to contend with. You *are* quite happy about Cathy marrying Stuart, aren't you?' Sam probed, watching her closely.

Too closely, Abbie acknowledged as she defensively turned her head away so that he couldn't look straight into her eyes.

'Cathy loves him,' she responded neutrally.

'Yes, she does, and he loves her,' Sam came back. 'So what's bothering you, Abbie?' he asked her, and then thoroughly undermined her determination not to confide in him by adding quietly, 'And don't bother denying that there is something. It might be one hell of a long time ago, but that doesn't alter the fact that there was a time when I knew every nuance of every expression that crossed your face—and what they meant.'

Had she really been so open to him? So vulnerable? Abbie wondered achingly. If so…

'Abbie,' Sam warned her.

'All right, if you must know, I'm concerned about Stuart's relationship with his mother—about the fact that she has such a strong influence over all her family.'

'Does she?' Sam looked unconvinced. 'I rather got the impression that Stuart was very much a young man who made his own decisions about his life. He loves Cathy and—'

'Yes, he loves her *now*,' Abbie agreed. 'But what if…what if there was ever a situation when Cathy needed to be able to rely on him, on his loyalty, on knowing that he would be strong enough to support her, to protect her, to…to love her no matter what or who?' she demanded passionately. 'What if—?'

'This isn't about Stuart and Cathy at all, is it?' Sam interrupted her roughly. 'It's about you and me. It's about what happened between us and the fact that in your eyes *I* did not have the loyalty, the strength, the trust to believe in you…'

'I don't want to talk about that…about us,' Abbie told him huskily. 'You say that Stuart and Cathy love one another, and I know that's true, but once you and I loved…*believed* we loved one another, and look what happened to us. It takes more, much more than just physical desire to build a strong marriage. After all,' she added bleakly, 'you and I both proved last night it is possible to desire someone, to want them, without…

'I don't want that for Cathy,' she told him, unable to finish what she had been about to say, all too aware of how precariously fragile her self-control was when it came to putting into words just how she felt about what had happened between them. 'I don't want her to have to wake up one morning and discover that the man she loves, the man she trusts…'

'Isn't very much of a man at all,' Sam supplied harshly for her when her voice faded into silence.

'I knew you wouldn't understand,' Abbie told him defiantly.

'On the contrary, I understand too well,' Sam responded grimly. 'But Stuart isn't me, Abbie, and Cathy isn't you, and they have to be left alone to take their own chances, make their own future. All we can do is give them our support and our love.'

'And you think that letting Cathy believe that we're getting back together is doing that?' Abbie challenged him.

'Yes,' Sam confirmed.

He was already halfway out of bed and Abbie quickly turned her head away, not wanting to watch him walk away from her, leave her. Last night everything had been so different, had seemed so right, but now, this morning, she was having to face the consequences of her own wilful refusal to see the truth.

As he saw the way Abbie turned her head, dismissing him from her line of sight in the same way she had dismissed him from her heart, Sam wondered why on earth he had ever hoped that last night could possibly have changed anything.

Yes, she was sexually responsive to him, and God knew he still wanted her, but then it was different for him; he wanted her *emotionally*—God, and how. Had she really not guessed how hard it had been for him to stop himself from telling her how he felt, how much he felt and for how long?

He'd been a fool, he acknowledged in self-derision, and not for the first time either. Last night he might have rekindled Abbie's desire for him, and her memories of how good their loving had once been, but this morning it was a very different set of memories he had evoked within her. This morning it was the pain he had caused her that was to the forefront of her mind, and not the pleasure they had once shared.

CHAPTER EIGHT

'WELL, you're a dark horse, aren't you?' Abbie winced as she heard the teasing note in Fran's voice. Her friend had telephoned a few seconds earlier, quite obviously having heard the news about Sam spending the night with her, and Abbie was glad that he had disappeared on business of his own and wasn't here to witness her flushed face and tear-filled eyes as Fran continued.

'Not that I'm totally surprised. *Despite* all your protests over the years I've always had a secret suspicion that a part of you still loved him. After all, the pair of you were so very, very much in love, and when you think about it it would have been impossible for those feelings to have been totally destroyed. It must have been so romantic, though, the two of you getting back together again... Just like being young again, only even better...

'Not that I'd be much good at romance a second time around—not with my cellulite and stretch marks,' Fran added ruefully. 'But you're more fortunate; you've still got a fabulous figure and—'

'A good figure or the lack of it doesn't have anything to do with having a good sex life,' Abbie felt bound to point out to her.

'No, maybe not, but it certainly helps banish a few of one's unwanted inhibitions,' Fran chuckled, adding forthrightly, 'Let's put it this way, I'd be far more interested in indulging in some playful bedroom gymnastics if I wasn't so hung up about my fat, wobbly bits. If you want my opinion, *that's* the advantage that a twenty-year-old really has over a forty-year-old. She can do it in any position she likes without worrying about her partner going into terminal shock at the sight of her un-clothed body. Everything stays where it should, whereas at our age…'

'We're in our forties, not our eighties, Fran,' Abbie reminded her dryly.

'So it was good, then?' Fran slipped in slyly. 'Only, according to what I've heard, when Cathy discovered the pair of you in bed together, you looked so exhausted you could barely summon the energy to lift your head off the pillow, and *Sam* looked like he was the first man to walk on the moon—'

'That wasn't exhaustion; that was embarrassment,' Abbie interrupted her forcefully, and then asked in a small voice, 'Where did you hear that—about Sam, I mean…?'

'In the supermarket,' Fran confessed cheerfully. 'You know that plump, pretty girl with the ponytail? Well, she told me…'

'Lesley,' Abbie supplied wrathfully. 'She's one of my temps. I'll kill her…'

'Why kill the messenger?' Fran quipped, and then added teasingly, 'And why feel embarrassed? I'll bet Sam isn't. I'll bet he—'

Quickly Abbie cut Fran off, fibbing untruthfully. 'Look. I've got to go.'

When she replaced the receiver Abbie was literally shaking, trembling physically with a mixture of anger and embarrassment—both emotions compounded by her feeling of the loss of any power to control what was happening to her, both internally and externally.

Fran's wasn't the only telephone call Abbie received from people plainly curious to discover what was going on. By mid-afternoon she had had enough, and was just about to take the phone off the hook when Cathy rang.

'Mum, at last—I've been trying to ring you for ages,' Cathy complained, but before Abbie could inform her just why she had not been able to get through, or take issue with her about the fact that so many people now seemed to have heard about her and Sam's 'reconciliation', Cathy continued excitedly, 'Stuart and I are going to see the house again, and we want you to come with us.

'The kitchen is a bit on the dark side,' Cathy confided, 'and I think it would look much better if we extended it and added on a small breakfast area-cum-conservatory, like you've done, but Stuart's worried that it might be too expensive. I've been telling him how much it would add to the value of the house. Oh, Mum, I'm dying for you to see it,' Cathy enthused. 'It's got so much potential.'

Abbie felt her original anger melting away as she listened to the warm excitement in Cathy's voice.

'I'd love to come with you,' she accepted. 'But I was just on my way to have a shower and get changed and I don't want to hold you up. Would it be easier for you if I met you there?'

'No, it's not a problem,' Cathy reassured her. 'We've got to go to the agent first anyway, to collect the keys, so we can call for you on the way back if that's okay.'

'Perfect,' Abbie confirmed.

All right, so Cathy had been rather thoughtless in the way she had broadcast the fact that she and Sam were supposedly back together again, but it *was* good to hear that special note of happiness in her daughter's voice and to share that special mother-daughter closeness with her, Abbie admitted ten minutes later as she stood under the shower, washing the foamy soap from her skin.

She had just stepped out of the shower and wrapped herself in a towel when she heard the kitchen door open.

'You can come up,' she called out. 'I'm almost ready.' Drying herself quickly, she discarded the towel and opened her dressing-table drawer to remove some clean underwear. She had just pulled on her briefs when she heard a tap on her bedroom door.

The small sound startled her a little. Cathy never normally knocked—just another indication of the fact that her daughter was growing up, and away from her!

'Come in, darling, there's no need to knock,' Abbie protested automatically.

Only it wasn't Cathy who pushed open the bedroom door and stood there surveying her semi-nude body and tangled hair. It was Sam.

Instinctively and ridiculously Abbie found that she was crossing her arms protectively over her bare breasts, her face, her whole body flushing betrayingly as she demanded shakily, 'What are *you* doing here? Where's Cathy?'

'She and Stuart have gone straight to the cottage; she asked me to come and pick you up. She was concerned that Stuart's parents might be there ahead of them, and she didn't want to keep them waiting.'

All the pleasure she had initially felt at the prospect of seeing the cottage faded as Abbie realised that it wasn't just Cathy, Stuart and herself who were going to see it.

'What do you mean? Cathy never said anything about anyone else going to see the house,' she protested. 'I thought it was just going to be us…me…' Even before she saw the unwanted compassion in Sam's eyes, Abbie knew that her voice and her face had both betrayed her feelings.

'I suspect that that *was* initially what Cathy intended,' Sam told her tactfully. 'But you know how these things escalate...'

'Oh, yes, I know,' Abbie agreed painfully. 'Oh, there's no need for you to look at me like that...I don't need you to feel sorry for me, Sam,' she told him angrily, adding abruptly, 'I've changed my mind about... about seeing the house. Please tell Cathy that I'll give her a ring and arrange to see it some other time.'

'No.'

'No?' As she repeated his calm, measured refusal to carry her message to Cathy, Abbie stared at him in angry confusion.

'You *can't* not go, Abbie,' she heard Sam informing her gently. 'Cathy wants you to be there; she's longing for you to see the house. She might be an adult but she still needs your love and approval.'

'Does she?' Abbie said bitterly. 'How do *you* know? Did Cathy *say* so to you?'

'She didn't need to,' Sam told her quietly. 'It's obvious to me how much you mean to her.'

'Is it? Well, it certainly isn't obvious to me, but then I was forgetting that as Cathy's *father* you no doubt have an insight into her thoughts and feelings denied to *me*.'

Even before she saw the swiftly hidden shocked compassion in Sam's eyes and heard his quiet, 'Abbie, what is it? What's wrong?' Abbie was cursing her betraying tongue, but it was too late.

Sam was already crossing the space between them, taking hold of her shoulders—her naked shoulders, Abbie realised as she tensed her body and dropped her hands to push him away. But her action came just seconds too late and she could already feel the warmth of his body through the cotton of the shirt he was wearing brushing against her naked breasts, sensitising her skin, which was already far, far too sensitive to the promise of the warm, male hardness of the body it could sense beneath the soft fabric of his shirt.

Abbie froze, afraid to move away from him, knowing that doing so would reveal to Sam the betraying hardness of her nipples. What was happening to her? Why on earth was she reacting to him like this? *Why* was her body remembering the physical intimacy between them as though it had been something special, something magical, something rare and to be treasured, when her brain had already told it over and over again that all it had been was mere physical lust?

'I've always had a secret suspicion that a part of you still loved him,' Fran had told her.

The panic she had felt on waking up in the morning and finding Sam in bed beside her returned. She remembered how it had felt to be back in his arms and knew that no matter how much she fought to deny it it was not just her body that had responded to him, and this time there was no avoiding the message it carried with it.

How *could* she still love Sam after what he had done, after the way he had hurt her? Had she no sense of self-preservation? Was it truly possible to separate the man from his crime? To love him whilst loathing what he had done and out of that love to…to what…? To forgive him? To go on loving him?

It *was* just sex. Just sex, that was all, Abbie told herself frantically. It wasn't possible for her still to love Sam. She didn't *want* to still love him, because if she did…if she did… Her body started to tremble, Sam's gentle restraining hold on her forgotten as the depth and intensity of her anguished thoughts and emotions claimed her. She could not still love Sam, she denied wretchedly, her body trembling in agitation, because if she did he would hurt her again, and this time…this time…

Before she'd had her youth and her need to protect her child on her side as her allies; now she had neither. Now she was too vulnerable.

'Abbie…Abbie, it's all right,' she heard Sam saying softly to her as he gathered her closer to his body, wrapping his arms around her as though…as though he *wanted* to hold her…as though he wanted to protect her…as though he actually cared about her and for her—which was totally impossible, Abbie reminded herself dizzily as she gave in to the temptation to let him hold and comfort her.

'I *do* understand how you feel…what you're going through, believe me,' she heard him telling her. 'Of course you feel hurt, angry…resentful—wary of Stuart's mother's influence over Cathy; but you're wrong to think that Cathy doesn't need you…that she doesn't value you.'

It was Cathy who he thought was responsible for her physical weakness, her vulnerability, Abbie recognised. He hadn't realised the effect that *he* was having on her, and she obviously couldn't possibly be having the same effect on him, she acknowledged wryly, otherwise there was no way he could continue to hold her virtually nude body in his arms without…without…

She gave a small swallow as she acknowledged the direction her thoughts, her desires were taking, knowing despairingly that if he were to close that small gap between their lower bodies and draw her even closer to him, if he were to slide his hands down over her naked back and kiss the exposed side of her throat, if he were to pick her up and carry her over to her bed, the bed they had shared only so very, very recently…

Thoroughly shaken by what she was experiencing, Abbie took a firm hold of her thoughts.

'Does she?' she questioned Sam quietly, forcing herself to look directly at him. 'Does she *really* value me, Sam? Would she continue to value me, do you think, if she knew the truth about what happened between us?' she asked him bitterly.

'You're not being fair to yourself, or to me,' Sam told her. 'What we had…what we did…' He frowned and looked away from her face. As she followed his sombre gaze Abbie saw him focusing briefly on her bare breasts and heard his indrawn breath, as though he hadn't actually realised until now that she was virtually naked.

'I can't go to the cottage. I can't go there knowing that she'll have told Stuart's parents, Stuart's mother about us…knowing what they'll be thinking.' Abbie panicked.

'Would you rather have them thinking about why we're *not* there?' Sam asked her throatily.

Abbie stared at him, frowning slightly, not understanding. He was, she recognised, quite definitely looking at her body now, and he was aware of it as well. He didn't, after all, need to close the gap between them for her to be aware of his arousal.

Men were so different from women in that way—able to be physically aroused by women they neither liked nor really wanted. Sam's physical arousal now was simply a male reaction to the sight of an unclad female body, she reminded herself; there was nothing personal about it. Nothing personal about the way his face was slightly flushed and his voice had dropped to a husky purr of male warmth.

'If we don't turn up at the cottage now they're all

going to think it's because we can't bear to tear ourselves away from our rediscovery of each other.'

'You're mad, they'll think we're…we're…'

'Making love,' Sam supplied softly for her.

'We can't let them think that,' Abbie protested, panicking. 'I must get dressed…'

As she looked wildly towards the bed, and the bra and dress laid out on it, Sam followed her gaze.

'Don't bother with the bra,' he told her softly. 'Just put on the dress; it will be quicker.'

'Quicker?' Abbie stared at him. She couldn't remember the last time she had neglected to wear her underwear. Her face suddenly flushed betrayingly. Yes, she could, and it had been at Sam's suggestion then, as it was now—although for far different reasons. Then her breasts had been firm and pert enough to get away with such behaviour, even if she had felt self-conscious. Now…

'I…I couldn't,' she started to protest, but Sam had released her and was walking over to the bed, picking up her dress. It was calf-length, a very respectable polished cotton frock in black, with a small cream motif and a row of tiny buttons all the way down the front. It was a dress she frequently wore for less formal business meetings—smart enough for her to look professional without appearing too intimidating. And she had certainly never ever—until she saw the way Sam was holding it, looking at those tiny buttons—envisaged it as being an outfit which possessed the least degree of sexual provocativeness.

'Everyone will know,' she protested, but her voice was a mere whisper of sound and she was already walking towards Sam, taking the dress from him and putting it on, instinctively turning her back to him as she tried to fasten the tiny buttons.

'No, they won't,' Sam reassured her, coming round to stand in front of her and pushing her shaking fingers out of the way whilst he completed the task for her.

Was it her imagination or did his fingers really linger over those few buttons whilst he closed the dress over her breasts?

'But *you'll* know,' Abbie protested, her voice registering her bewilderment that she could behave in such a way, that she could so tamely and easily give in to what he was suggesting.

'Oh, yes, *I'll* know,' Sam agreed, and this time she was certainly not imagining it as he gently ran the pad of his thumb over one erect nipple and then bent to kiss the bared valley between her breasts before he finished closing all the buttons.

At least the cream jacket she habitually wore over the dress gave her *some* degree of additional protection and concealment, Abbie reflected as she slipped on her shoes and hurried out of the bedroom. And with any luck Cathy and the others might have got so tired of waiting for them that they would have gone!

Only of course they had not. They were still there. And Stuart's mother, frowning over the blowsy untidiness of the cottage's garden, was predictably the first to see them as they arrived. The smile with which she welcomed Sam was markedly warmer than the smile with which she welcomed her, Abbie noticed as she resolutely tried to hide her own feelings and display a warmth towards the other woman which she found it hard to genuinely feel.

At the most there couldn't be more than twelve or so years between them, Abbie reflected, but Stuart's mother always made her feel more like a naughty schoolgirl than a responsible fellow adult.

'I was *so* glad to hear Cathy's news—that you and

her father have managed to resolve your…problems,' she told Abbie in a confidential whisper as Sam turned aside to talk with Stuart's father. 'I know, of course, that separation and even divorce are quite the norm these days, but when it comes to an occasion such as a wedding one is always conscious of the problems they can give rise to.

'Are you actually planning to remarry before Stuart and Catherine?' she asked. 'I expect you will be going together anyway,' she went on, whilst Abbie stared at her in a speechless mixture of anger and shock. 'It will look so much better on the invitations, won't it?' she was continuing, apparently oblivious of the pink flags of temper flying warningly in Abbie's otherwise pale face.

'Catherine tells me that she's considering having the wedding breakfast at Ladybower. It is a delightful venue, although personally I always think there's something so much more personal about a wedding breakfast held in one's own grounds.'

'I'm sure,' Abbie managed to grate out between gritted teeth. 'But unfortunately the ''grounds'' surrounding my home—' Out of the corner of her eye Abbie could see Cathy, who had come to join Sam and Stuart's father, biting down hard on her lip and looking anxious, and so, instead of completing the defensively sardonic comment she had started to utter, Abbie reminded herself that her daughter's happiness was a far more important thing than her own pride and said quietly instead, 'The cottage garden is far too small to hold a marquee, unfortunately. Have you seen round the house yet?' she asked, making a heroic effort to be pleasant and avoid any contentious issues.

'Oh, yes, we were the first to see it. Stuart wanted his father's opinion straight away.'

His father's opinion or his mother's approval? Abbie wondered bitterly.

'It's a good size, and well built,' Stuart's mother continued, before adding dismissively, 'It *is* a semi-detached, though. Stuart's father feels he's got off very lightly. Neither of our girls would settle for anything less than a detached—but then, of course, I suppose it all depends on what you've been used to. I must say, I found the rooms dreadfully poky, but then I suppose Catherine will be used to that.'

Mortified by the hot flood of angry tears burning the back of her eyes at hearing the home she had so lovingly provided for her daughter so disparaged, Abbie had to turn away...inside her jacket pockets her hands were balled into two small fists.

Mentally she willed her daughter, who she knew must have overheard the comment, to come to her defence, but Cathy had turned her back on her and was talking very quickly and energetically to Stuart's father about their plans to extend the kitchen and to add a new garage and a laundry room to the side of the house.

'I always think it's a mistake to do too much to this kind of property,' Stuart's mother was saying. 'They do have a ceiling value, and, as I've already said to Stuart, now that the girls are gone there's really no reason why he and Catherine shouldn't move in with us for a little while, whilst they save up and look around for something a little more suit—a little bit larger.'

Now it was Cathy's turn to look imploringly at *her*, Abbie saw, her heart aching at the tension and anxiety she could see in her daughter's face, and she denied quickly, 'Oh, no, that—'

'That's a wonderfully generous offer, Anne.' Sam interrupted Abbie calmly, smiling warmly in Stuart's mother's direction. 'Especially as both you and George must be looking forward to having some time on your own together. However, personally I don't think it does any harm at all for young people to have to struggle a little bit—as I'm sure that you and George must have done when you were first married.'

As Abbie looked on in mingled anger and astonishment she saw Stuart's mother responding to Sam's subtle flattery like a cat being stroked, the look she gave him in response to his comment both slightly arch and complacent.

'Well, yes, we did both have to work very hard,' she agreed. 'George's parents had a huge house in those days, but George was the first to leave home and there was certainly no question of us being invited to make our home with them. No, we had to do it the hard way...'

'And look at the success you've made of your lives,' Sam told her warmly. 'An example which I'm sure that Stuart and Cathy both want to emulate. You mustn't spoil them too much,' he added outrageously—or so at least Abbie thought. Was she the only one who was aware of what he was doing? she wondered indignantly as she saw the way Stuart's mother bridled and patted her hair betrayingly. 'Otherwise I shall be forced to do the same, and before we know it the pair of them will be playing one of us off against the other.'

'Oh, no, Stuart would never do anything like that,' Stuart's mother denied immediately, leaping to her son's defence. Her son's—not *her* daughter's, Abbie noticed bitterly.

'However, you do have a point,' she conceded graciously, still smiling at Sam. 'And George *has* been talking about the two of us doing some travelling once he's retired. I still think they could do better than this, though,' she added frowningly. 'The kitchen especially is so poky and dark—although I don't expect that matters too much these days. Just so long as there's room for a freezer and a microwave, modern girls don't seem to worry too much.'

Modern girls. Abbie drew in a seething breath, itching to demand, What about modern boys? But as though he guessed what she was thinking…what she was wanting to say… Sam suddenly turned his head and looked warningly at her, giving his head a small shake.

It irked Abbie unbearably that he should have been the one to rescue Cathy from the threat of having to live with her prospective mother-in-law and not her, and she was sorely tempted to ignore Sam's warning look and give vent to her ire, but common sense told her that the person who would suffer the most if she did would be Cathy, and so instead she turned to her daughter and, summoning all her will-power, said as naturally as she could, 'Come on, then, darling, show me round…'

'I'd take off that jacket first, if I were you,' Stuart's mother warned her. 'The house is very dusty. I always think that cream is such an impractical colour; navy is so much more useful.'

Abbie didn't make any response; she was too busy trying to conceal her dismay at the way Stuart's father had stepped forward courteously to help her off with her jacket. 'Don't bother with the bra,' Sam had murmured suggestively, and God alone knew why she had witlessly done as he had asked.

Stuart and his father might not notice that her breasts were bare beneath their thin covering of cotton, but she hadn't a hope in hell of concealing the fact from her sharp-eyed daughter without the protection of her jacket, Abbie acknowledged, her heart sinking as she reluctantly and uncomfortably allowed Stuart's father to relieve her of it.

The temptation to cross her arms protectively in front of her chest, as she had done when Sam had walked so unexpectedly into her bedroom, was one she only just managed to resist. Cathy had already done a brief wide-eyed double take as she glanced at her mother and then looked back again, her eyes rounding sightly. As Abbie felt her face start to burn with openly embarrassed colour, Sam calmly detached himself from Stuart's father's side and walked over towards her, standing somehow so that the bulk of his body threw her own into its protective shadow, making her feel at once both relieved and somehow safer. Relieved...? Safer...? With Sam? Impossible.

'Are we going to go in the front door formally or the back door as family?' she heard Sam teasing Cathy as he put his hand on his ex-wife's arm and guided her towards the house, just as though for all the world they were genuinely a couple, just as though they *were* actually...together...reconciled...a pair...lovers...

Abbie swallowed painfully, unable to look directly either at Sam or anyone else, but most especially not at Sam. What was she afraid he might see in her eyes? she asked herself fiercely, but she already knew it was a question she could not bring herself to answer.

Half an hour later, when she and Cathy were alone in the house's small dark kitchen, Abbie touched her daughter gently on the arm and told her comfortingly, 'Don't worry about Stuart's mother's criticisms, darling. I think this house has an awful lot of potential.'

To her chagrin, Cathy shrugged away from her, telling her curtly, 'Stuart's mother *isn't* criticising; she's just trying to be helpful. And I wish that you... *Will* you and Dad be getting remarried before our wedding?' Cathy asked, changing the subject.

Still trying to deal with the hurt Cathy's initial rejection of her own opinion and support of Stuart's mother had caused her, Abbie couldn't trust herself to speak.

'Your mother and I haven't made any concrete plans yet, but when we do you'll be the first to hear about them.'

Abbie whirled round. She hadn't heard Sam come into the kitchen. For such a big man, he was disconcertingly light-footed.

'You won't forget that we're expecting you for lunch, will you?' Stuart's mother reminded Sam archly as she too entered the kitchen.

'No, we'll both be there,' Sam promised her, whilst Abbie held her breath. Surely Sam must have realised, just as she had, that the invitation had been extended only to *him*?

But Stuart's mother was now acknowledging Abbie's new role in Sam's life, her smile slightly forced as she concurred a little too heartily, 'Yes, of course—both of you. That will be lovely.'

It was Cathy who put the final blot of misery on Abbie's afternoon as she walked her parents to Sam's car, taking advantage of the fact that Sam was deep in conversation with Stuart to hiss angrily to Abbie, 'I appreciate how things are between you and Dad, Mum, but you might have…have dressed properly. I mean, that kind of thing looks so tacky…especially at your age…and Stuart's mother is bound to have noticed.'

As she and Sam walked towards the car Abbie wasn't sure what emotion she felt the most strongly—pain or anger.

CHAPTER NINE

ABBIE sat in silence next to Sam as he drove her home, saying only when he had stopped the car outside her cottage, 'Thank you. There's no need for you to come in with me...'

'We do have rather a lot to discuss,' Sam pointed out.

'Like what?' Abbie demanded. 'The kind of clothes Cathy expects me to wear when we have lunch with Stuart's parents?'

Sam looked at her gravely.

'That was my fault and I'm sorry, even though the sight of those deliciously feminine breasts of yours was the only enjoyable part of an otherwise thoroughly unenjoyable outing.'

'If you're trying to blame me for that—' Abbie began aggressively.

'I'm not blaming anyone,' Sam soothed her. 'But it's obvious that Anne feels very much in awe of you—and that, in turn, makes both Stuart and Cathy overly protective of her.'

'She's in awe of *me*?' Abbie spluttered. 'How on earth do you work that one out? All she did practically all afternoon was criticise me and try to put me down...?

To her irritation she saw that Sam was smiling at her.

'Oh, come on, Abbie,' he challenged her. 'You're far too intelligent, far too good a judge of character to be taken in by such defensive behaviour. You must have asked yourself why she is so defensive.

'Look at it from her point of view. All she's done

with her life is stay at home looking after her husband and raising her children, whilst you—'

'She thinks I'm a dreadful mother...that I've neglected Cathy and put my own needs first,' Abbie protested, but Sam was shaking his head.

'No, that's what she tries to pretend she thinks,' he told her firmly, 'but in reality it's very obvious to see that she's terrified of losing Cathy and Stuart to you and your influence over their lives.'

'What? That's ridiculous,' Abbie objected.

'Is it?' Sam asked her, adding firmly, 'Look, let's continue this discussion inside. As I've already said, there are several things we need to talk about...'

'Such as?' Abbie demanded ungraciously, even whilst she was inwardly acknowledging that he was quite right.

He opened his car door and came round to open hers for her.

After the drab disuse and forlorn emptiness of Cathy and Stuart's prospective first home, the warm cheerfulness of Abbie's kitchen was strikingly apparent. Sam glanced round it appreciatively and told her with genuine admiration, 'You always did have a special gift for turning a house into a home.'

'I wouldn't call it a special gift,' Abbie denied. 'It's something that's almost second nature to a lot of women, I believe. In the way that some men are attracted to tinkering with anything mechanical,' she added wryly.

'Ah, yes, the coffee percolator,' Sam agreed with a grin. 'That was a mistake, I admit...'

'A mistake? It was rather more than that when it exploded, covering the kitchen we'd just decorated in wet coffee grounds,' Abbie corrected him. Her mouth had started to twitch into a smile which very quickly became a giggling bubble of laughter.

Across the kitchen their eyes met as both of them

remembered the incident, a small scene from the first days of their marriage.

Abbie had cried at first when she had seen the devastation the exploding coffee pot had wreaked on her new kitchen, but Sam had assured her that no lasting damage had been done and she had guilelessly allowed him to draw her upstairs away from the scene of devastation to 'check that there's no damage up there'.

There hadn't been, of course, but once upstairs it had been an easy task for Sam to coax her into their bedroom.

He had claimed, she remembered, that the coffee grounds he had licked off her skin had had the most delicious and aphrodisiac flavour.

She shook her head ruefully now.

'It honestly wasn't my fault. The percolator was quite definitely faulty,' Sam complained.

'It certainly was,' Abbie agreed, fresh laughter gurgling in her throat and lightening her eyes.

'So I made a misjudgement…a mistake,' Sam conceded with a mock-injured air. 'Everyone's allowed one mistake.'

'One mistake.' The laughter died from Abbie's eyes. She, it seemed, had made far more than one mistake and misjudgement where her daughter was concerned… Too many for the gulf which had developed between Cathy and herself ever to be properly bridged.

'What is it…what's wrong?' Sam asked her quietly, watching the pain replace the earlier happiness and amusement in her eyes.

'I was just thinking that some mistakes can't be forgotten or forgiven,' Abbie told him curtly, turning her head away so that he couldn't look properly at her, suddenly annoyed with herself for being vulnerable and emotional enough to admit her fears to him.

Why should he care if Cathy turned away from her? As far as *he* was concerned, such an occurrence could only be to his benefit. She was a fool to let him see what she was thinking...what she was feeling. She was a fool to have let him come in with her in the first place.

'Abbie, if you're referring to what happened between us, I know that—'

'Between *us*?' Abbie cut in sharply, shaking her head, her voice thickening with tears as she told him, 'No...I was talking about Cathy...about the mistakes I've made with her, the misjudgements.'

She couldn't help it. She knew her emotions were going to get the better of her. *Why* was this happening to her, to her of all women, when she had always so determinedly refused to give in to her emotions in public, when no matter how desperately unhappy she had felt she had kept her tears for the privacy of her own solitude and her pillow?

'The mistakes you've made with Cathy?' Sam was frowning at her now, his voice concerned. 'Abbie, you haven't. You've been an exemplary mother...an exemplary parent. Look, why don't you go and sit down in the sitting room? I'll make us both a hot drink and we can talk the whole thing through...'

'What good will talking about it do?' Abbie protested, but she was already turning towards the inner door and opening it, walking through it and into her small pretty sitting room with its French windows overlooking the garden.

It had gone dark enough for her to need to switch on the lamps—the overhead light would be too harsh, too revealing—and it was cool enough for her to welcome the heat from her gas flame fire.

Because the room was so small she had decorated it in natural colours and fibres—soft cream cottons and hessian, her junk shop find of a heavy old Chesterfield sofa re-covered in a cream damask fabric she had bought at a bargain price because it had a small flaw.

She had finished re-covering it just in time for Cathy's eighteenth birthday, and she remembered how proud she had felt at the small adults-only party she had given to celebrate the occasion, when Cathy had praised her cleverness.

'The cleverest thing I've ever done was producing you,' she had told her daughter lovingly then—and she had meant it. She still felt it. The cleverest and the best. And it hurt to know that all her shining pride and love in her daughter was something that Cathy found more of a burden than a joy.

She embarrassed Cathy, she decided as she curled herself up into a small mock-foetal ball on the sofa, kicking off her shoes to tuck her feet up underneath her—something she only did when she was feeling particularly vulnerable and unhappy. Cathy would much rather have had a mother like Stuart's. A mother whose name would not have to stand glaringly alone on her wedding invitations. A mother who was the living proof of the solid security in which she had brought up her family. A mother whose photograph collection included a silver-framed photograph of her wedding and alongside it another of her silver wedding; that was the kind of mother Cathy wanted, not the kind like her, minus a marriage, a husband and her underwear.

A small sob of mingled misery and guilt hiccuped past Abbie's lips into the silence of the small room, causing Sam, who had just walked in, to pause and glance at her frowningly before carefully depositing the two mugs of coffee he had been carrying onto a small covered side table.

'Abbie, you can't really believe that Cathy would

have preferred to have a mother like Anne,' he chided her gently as he sat down beside her and took hold of her hands before she could stop him, holding them warmly in his own.

'Can't I?' she demanded, once again amazed by Sam's apparent ability to read her mind, and inwardly acknowledging that it would be undignified and no doubt impossible to try to pull her hands free of Sam's warm male grip.

'You're everything that any child could want in a mother,' he continued, the intensity of his voice making her forget his unauthorised hold on her hands and look directly into his eyes to search for some sign that he was secretly being sarcastic about her; but there was none.

'You've done so much, achieved so much...'

'Have I?' Abbie questioned tiredly. Tears sparkled emotionally in her eyes. She tried to raise her hand to dash them away and then realised that Sam was still holding it.

As her fear of her own emotions swamped her she cried out fiercely, 'Let me go, Sam...'

'I wish I could,' Sam responded thickly. 'I wish to God I could.'

And then, before she could stop him, he was drawing her closer to him, kissing first one and then the other of her captive hands, and then each damp eyelid which she had squeezed shut defensively against both her own threatening tears and the sight of Sam so intimately close to her.

It was his fault that all this was happening to her, his fault that she no longer seemed to be in full control of her life, his fault that her emotions were being stirred and aroused as they hadn't been in years—his fault that right now, instead of stiffening her body against him and thoroughly and completely rejecting him, she was actually snuggling closer to him, her mouth softening in aching longing beneath the warm caress of his.

Her hands were free now as he encircled her in his arms, drawing her so close to him that she was virtually sitting in his lap, body to body with him, and her hands, the hands she *should* have used to push him away, instead reached out to hold him.

'We shouldn't be doing this...'

She heard herself say the words and knew as easily as Sam quite obviously did that they were nothing more than a trite sop to convention, lacking any real meaning or vehemence. *That* was all being expressed via her body language, the body language that had her leaning into Sam's body, her hands somehow or other having made their way up under his shirt to cling to the solid, hard-packed muscles of his back, whilst she tipped back her head in feminine enticement to the growing urgency of his mouth and he caressed the soft skin of her throat.

Already Abbie could feel her body responding to him, welcoming him, wanting him, its needs far too turbulently strong and demanding for her mind to control or suppress.

The knowledge of how much she wanted him shocked her into silence, unable to resist or protest as Sam slowly started to unfasten the buttons on her dress, lingeringly kissing every inch of flesh he exposed.

Why was she behaving so recklessly, so...so dangerously? Surely only a woman in love could behave like this, a woman motivated and driven by love?

Love. Abbie felt the shudder of self-knowledge start right down in her toes and work its way through her whole body, as electrifying and jaggedly painful as the fiercest of forked lightning, jerking her body in a visible spasm of rejection, making her cry out a harshly guttural denial and causing Sam to lift his hand to cup her face, his thumb-tip stroking lovingly against her skin as he asked roughly, 'What is it? What's wrong?'

What was wrong?

Abbie closed her eyes against the hot wash of her self-betraying tears. Everything was wrong. How could it not be when she was so incapable of correctly analysing a situation, a man's touch, that she mistook what could only be unemotional physical desire for loving tenderness? When she was so incapable of honestly facing up to and recognising her own feelings that it had taken her until now, until this, to truly understand that the anger, the hatred, the loathing of Sam which she had nurtured for so many years had simply been a sham, feelings she had forced herself to believe she felt as a form of self-protection.

She didn't hate Sam, she acknowledged despairingly, she loved him. But he didn't love her. Even if her foolish heart and her even more foolish mind wanted to believe that he did.

'Abbie, please don't cry, my love. I can't bear to see your tears…I can't bear seeing you hurt…'

She could hear Sam's words, feel his gentle touch on her face as he brushed away her tears, but she felt too numb with shock, too caught up in the pain of self-discovery, to really register what he was saying, what he was doing—until she felt his mouth cover her own.

It was gentle at first, but then quickened with such urgency, such hungry desire and need for her that all her good intentions were swept away by the knowledge of how much she loved and wanted him in return, and how precious and fleeting this bittersweet intimacy with him could only be, so that before she could stop herself she was returning the urgency of his kiss, a woman now, not a girl, her body knowing the pleasure he could give it, knowing the pleasure *she* could give him.

Later, she would acknowledge that it might have been Sam who unfastened the rest of her dress, but she was certainly the one who shrugged herself free of it, baring her naked, swollen breasts to the warmth of the fire and the even greater heat of Sam's smouldering visual caress of her gleaming skin and dark rose nipples.

And she certainly needed no encouragement to arch her back and offer their sensual enticement to his eager hands and lips as she silently, and then not so silently, urged him to stroke and suckle at her eagerly sensitive nipples. Her fingers rhythmically kneaded the hard bones of his skull, burrowing into the thick darkness of his hair as she held him against her breast and whispered huskily disjointed phrases of pleasure and desire.

At some point she must have told him that she wanted his body to be as physically accessible to her as hers was to him, although she had no recollection of doing so, because he paused in the midst of kissing her and then, with his mouth still on hers, started to unfasten his shirt with one hand, the other still cupping the side of her face, his fingers stroking her skin as though he was unable to bear the thought of not touching her.

One of the things which had both shocked and excited her when she and Sam had first become lovers had been the way he refused to either close his eyes or allow her to close hers, insisting that they maintain eye contact with one another. He didn't want them to shut themselves away from one another behind closed eyelids, he had told her then, and now, as though her body was still responding to him as it had done all those years ago, she found it impossible to keep her eyes closed, impossible not to look at him, so that as she saw him tugging impatiently at his shirt buttons on the periphery of her vision she could feel her face, her whole body starting to flood with heat as she registered his impatience.

In the end she had to help him. It was either that or risk him ripping the buttons free and ruining his shirt, she told herself in extenuation of her own illogical behaviour. But then she *had* been the one to whisper that she wanted to see him, to touch him, to feel his skin next to her own, she admitted, her face flushing even more hotly as Sam reminded her throatily of just what she had said, placing his palm against hers, twining his fingers with hers as he carried her hand to his body and placed it over his heat.

This couldn't be happening, Abbie denied dizzily, not to her and not with Sam, and not like this. This was the stuff of the most sensual and romantic fantasies—every woman's dream come true. To be touched, held, caressed, to be slowly and deliciously made love to by a man, *the* man, who only had to so much as look at her in that certain way to make her whole body melt.

No wonder, in the years they had been apart, she had never delved too deeply into just why she had found it so impossible to be sexually responsive to any other man. Her body had known the truth even if her mind had ignored and denied it.

Quickly she broke their kiss, no longer able to sustain the intimacy of their shared eye contact, afraid that Sam might read in her eyes what she now knew was written across and deep, deep into her heart.

As she caressed the smooth, damp column of his throat with her lips she knew it wasn't just passion that was making her heart thud so frantically.

She heard Sam groan as she licked the sweat from the hollow at the base of his throat. He groaned even more harshly when she teasingly circled his nipple with the tip of her finger and then very gently licked and then sucked first one and then the other.

'Now you know what it feels like when you do it to

me,' she told him boldly, watching the muscles in his throat grow rigid and the sweat streak his already damp skin.

'What about you?' Sam challenged her thickly. 'Do *you* know how it feels when you touch me? How *I* feel? How you make me feel, the things you make me want to do?'

Whilst she watched him, dizzily aware of the high-octane sensual excitement he was deliberately building inside her, knowing that what he was saying to her was as sexually exciting for her as it obviously was for him, he took hold of her, removing her clothes completely, and then, before she could stop him, he bent his head and gently kissed the soft curve of her stomach.

'I'm sorry, I'm sorry... I'm sorry I didn't believe you,' Abbie heard him telling her huskily. 'I wish to God I had, Abbie. I wish to God things had been different, that I hadn't rejected you and Cathy.'

His voice had thickened betrayingly, and as he leaned his face against her stomach Abbie could feel her skin growing damp, and then he lifted his head and looked at her, showing her the visible signs of his emotion and remorse. The tears he was too much of a man to want to conceal from her.

Abbie's heart suddenly ached with answering emotion. Instinctively she reached out and wrapped her arms around his shoulders.

'You had what you believed were good reasons for not believing me,' she heard herself saying, and recognised, on a sudden surge of shock, that she genuinely meant it, that for the first time it *was* possible for her not just to admit but to genuinely appreciate *why* he had refused to believe that Cathy was his child.

'No reason could ever have been good enough to make me doubt or question you,' she heard him telling her gruffly. 'I should have trusted you…believed you…'

'You'd had a vasectomy,' Abbie reminded him. 'As far as you were concerned it was impossible for me to have conceived your child…'

'You say that as though you mean it,' Sam told her sombrely. 'I can't ask you for forgiveness, Abbie—how can you ever forgive me when *I* can't forgive myself? And forgiveness can't wipe out all the years of pain that lie between us, can it? I'm a human being, and flawed. But, like everyone else, I want to be accepted…loved *with* my imperfections, not in spite of them.

'But we shouldn't be discussing this now. In fact we shouldn't be doing any talking whatsoever now,' he told her, his voice changing, slowing and thickening as he bent his head and kissed her stomach again. But this time his mouth was moving lower, and despite her cerebral desire to stop him, to tell him that there was no point, no future in what they were doing, her body was already responding to what he was doing to it.

She could feel herself starting to tremble as her self-control wavered and faltered, swept out of the way by the sweet sensuality of his mouth's increasingly intimate seduction of her, as though his mouth knew as it redis-covered her, recognising all the tiny involuntary signs that told it how much what it was doing, pleasured her, how much it was making her want him. Familiarity did not always breed contempt, Abbie recognised dizzily as a torrent of aching need swamped her. Sometimes it ig-nited a fire that burned so hotly, so intensely, that it threatened…

She gave a small anguished gasp of unendurable ec-stasy as Sam's mouth fastened gently over the most sen-sitive part of her.

She had no awareness, no recognition, of calling out

his name, of begging him, pleading with him to fill her with his body and to go on filling her until they were both complete and sated, but she knew she must have done so from the response he made to her.

All she did know was that the second time her body exploded into the convulsive rhythm of her orgasm Sam shared that release with her. Shared it and praised her for it, lavishing kisses and tender words of appreciation on her, stroking her skin, holding her close to his body, wrapping her tightly against him long, long after the climax of their shared pleasure had subsided.

It was only when she was on the verge of falling asleep in his arms that he finally moved, whispering softly to her, 'If I stay here much longer, we're both going to fall asleep, and the last thing we need now is to be found by our daughter again tomorrow morning—especially—'

Abbie stared at him in distress, interrupting him.

'You're leaving? But…' Quickly she bit her lip. What had she been expecting? That he would stay again? That they would go upstairs together, sleep together, just as though the last twenty-odd years had never happened—just as though they were, in fact, still married…still a couple?

'You want me to stay?' Sam questioned her.

Abbie shook her head. The last thing she needed right now was for him to guess how she felt. It was obvious that so far as he was concerned all he felt for her was a very male and unemotional kind of physical desire, a residue of lust from the past, no doubt. Whereas she…

'No. No, of course not. I was just…'

Quickly she turned away from him and started to pull on her clothes, suddenly feeling cold and self-conscious. But the outer chill of her exposed skin was nothing when compared with the inner iciness tightening its grip on her newly exposed and vulnerable heart.

Sam, too, was getting dressed, and as he stood up he turned to look at her and said hesitantly, 'You know, Abbie, it might not be such a bad idea of Cathy's...our getting married again. If only...'

'Why? Because it would look better on the wedding invitations?' Abbie asked him as she fiercely blinked away the tears of her pain.

'Is that the only reason you can think of?' he asked her quickly.

'Well, it would certainly make life a lot easier for Cathy, and for Stuart's mother,' Abbie told him jerkily. 'Unfortunately, I'm not as selfless as you, Sam. For me to ever marry again I would have to know that I loved and was loved in return, so deeply and so *completely* that nothing, no one—' She stopped, unable to go on.

'I hear what you're saying, Abbie,' Sam told her grimly. 'Don't worry, I get the message. You'd never want to marry me again because you couldn't trust me not to let you down again. Right?

'Oh, it's okay. I'm all grown-up now, and I've had to learn some hard lessons along the way. You don't have to explain to me that a fully mature woman has her needs and the right to satisfy them when and where she wishes, without her partner expecting her to swear undying love for him. I apologise if I let my emotions carry me away somewhat. Another good reason for not staying the night,' he added savagely. 'By morning I'd probably be—'

He didn't complete whatever it was he had been about to say, turning and heading for the door instead, pausing only to remind her, 'For Cathy's sake we've got to see this thing through, but I imagine as far as we're *both* concerned the sooner she and Stuart get married and the sooner you and I can go our separate ways the better.'

There were a dozen or more things she could have said to him, Abbie acknowledged after she had listened to the final sound of his car engine fading away. A dozen or so sharp retorts that would have reminded him that this whole stupid idea of them going along with Cathy's misconception that they were reconciled had been *his* and not hers, but the shock of the harshness of their quarrel, coming so quickly after the shared intimacy of their lovemaking, caught her with all her defences down, too vulnerable to withstand the pain she was feeling, never mind fight back.

And the worst thing of all, she admitted an hour later as she curled herself into a small, miserable ball beneath her duvet and hugged her pillow, was that if Sam were somehow miraculously to materialise here in bed beside her right now she would...she would... As the tears flowed unchecked down her face she gave vent to all her pent-up anguish and heartache with a sobbed female howl of pure misery.

CHAPTER TEN

ABBIE sighed. Tonight she and Sam were due to attend a dinner party given by Stuart's mother. Abbie didn't want to go, but she knew how Cathy would react if she tried to back out.

She had tried to talk to Cathy about the loss of the closeness they had always shared, but it was obvious that she had still not been forgiven for what Cathy saw as her mother's bad behaviour during her visit to see the house.

'I know that you and Dad are back together again, and I realise that you must...' Cathy had begun when Abbie had tried to talk to her about what had happened. 'But can't you see, Mum, that...well, that...that some things are just...inappropriate?'

'She's embarrassed and confused, and angry with herself for feeling like that,' Sam had announced promptly, when he had finally coaxed Abbie to admit what was bothering her. 'The visible signs of a parent's sexuality can be embarrassing to their teenage and adult offspring...'

'Even these days?' Abbie had protested in disbelief.

'Even these days,' Sam had told her. 'Especially when, like Cathy, an adult offspring has not grown up accepting and seeing his or her parents' shared physical love for one another.'

'She didn't seem embarrassed the morning she found us in bed together,' Abbie had pointed out.

'No, but then she was probably too euphoric to be aware of anything other than her delight in the fact that we were reconciled. Now it's rather different. Don't worry about it,' he had advised Abbie. 'She'll come round once she's had time to get used to the idea. She's an intelligent girl and she's bound to be aware of the ambivalence and contradiction of how she's feeling.'

'She was right, though,' Abbie had felt bound to admit. 'I shouldn't have gone out like that. Not when...'

'Not when what?' Sam had interposed softly, with a look in his eyes which had made Abbie's heart thump heavily—and not with apprehension either. No, certainly not with that. 'Not when you have breasts perfectly made to arouse every single one of a man's senses? Soft, warm, deliciously scented, heavenly to touch and even more heavenly to taste, to suckle—so sensual and desirable in every way that just knowing the effect they have—'

'Sam, stop it,' Abbie had protested shakily, and then wondered why it was, when they were both so extraordinarily sensually responsive to one another, when she dreaded each and every second she had to spend with him, once he was actually there, being with him came as easily and naturally as breathing. And then she remembered why they couldn't turn the charade they were enacting into reality.

Tonight's dinner party was going to be particularly difficult; Anne was bound to question her about her and Sam's plans, to ask—as she had done before—if Abbie had yet come to a decision about selling her own house, and if so would they look for somewhere here in town or move closer to the university.

'They've offered me the Senior Chair,' Sam had told her abruptly three evenings ago, when he had called round unannounced, just as Abbie was preparing her supper. Naturally she had felt obliged to ask him to stay.

'Are you going to accept it?' she had challenged him.

She had tried to protest about the number of times he'd either called round or telephoned, but he had simply reminded her, 'Cathy will think it off if I don't.'

'You might just as well be living here,' she had exploded only two days ago, when he had arrived just after she had had a particularly stressful afternoon at work.

His soft, 'Is that an invitation?' had shocked her into silence, her mind screaming that, no, the last thing she needed now was the added strain of having him living under her roof whilst her emotions and her body...

She tensed, not wanting to acknowledge just how it had felt to let herself imagine how it would be if they were living together, how it would feel to share that very special intimacy with him again, to wake up in the morning curled up into his body, knowing that he was a *permanent* part of her life.

'Do you want me to?' he had asked her in answer to her tense challenge about his future plans.

He was standing far too close to her as he waited for her response, Abbie had acknowledged as she'd wetted her nervously dry lips with her tongue-tip, wishing that there were some way she could conceal her expression from him.

In the end all she could manage was a stiff, 'Your future plans don't have anything to do with me. Cathy's the one you should be consulting.'

She had seen the way his eyes darkened as he took in that brief, betraying dampening touch of her tongue to her mouth, and her own body had responded dangerously to the sensual message of his awareness. Being close to him was like being physically drugged or drunk, she'd decided as she'd tried to fight off the effects of the way he made her feel.

'After all,' she hadn't been able to resist adding recklessly, 'she's the one you're doing all of this for, the one you're doing all the pretending for, making this sacrifice for.'

Ridiculously she'd held her breath slightly, almost as though she was actually being foolish enough to hope that he would deny it and tell her... Tell her what?

'It really doesn't matter to me what decision you come to,' she had finished carelessly, and untruthfully, finally managing to turn away from him as she delivered the words, reinforcing them with a small, dismissive shrug.

'No... No, it doesn't, does it?' Sam had agreed quietly.

He had left shortly afterwards without finishing his supper—probably because he wanted to call round and tell Cathy his news, Abbie had decided. And she had refused to give in to the temptation to run to her sitting-room window and watch him drive away.

Sam arrived, as Abbie had known he would, on the dot of eight to pick her up. Since Anne, as she herself put it, 'liked to do things properly', dinner was to be a formal affair, and Abbie's vulnerable heart missed a beat as she recognised how very malely attractive Sam looked in his dinner jacket.

She herself was wearing a softly tailored, fine wool crêpe trouser suit, and to her irritation she realised that she was actually blushing slightly as she saw the way that Sam was looking at her, and the approval in his eyes.

'You always were a stunningly pretty girl, Abbie,' he told her sincerely. 'But now, as a woman—'

'As a woman I do not either appreciate or need falsely flattering compliments,' Abbie interrupted him curtly, but her pulse was beating far too fast and she could not quite bring herself to look directly into his eyes.

'No, I don't imagine you do,' Sam agreed gravely.

'Nor do I deceive myself that I'm the first and only man to recognise how beautifully and serenely you've grown into your womanhood, Abbie, nor how much, how very, very much, it becomes you…'

Before Abbie could take issue with him on his choice of the word 'serene' to describe her, Sam was continuing softly, 'You wear it well, Abbie. You wear it very well indeed. The girl I married was heart-wrenchingly pretty, but the woman you've become…'

He gave a tiny shake of his head. 'It's quite true what they say about true beauty being much, much more than skin-deep. Yours shines out of you, Abbie; it illuminates you and everyone around.'

'We…we're going to be late,' was all Abbie could manage to say. In another man she might almost have thought his words were dictated by cruel malice, in the knowledge of how she felt, but that was something she could never accuse Sam of. He would never deliberately, knowingly inflict pain on anyone and then stand back to observe their agony.

It was some small consolation, she supposed, that he had no idea of how she actually felt—a swab to staunch any wound to her pride. But what was the point in attending to any small lacerations in that whilst emotionally she was haemorrhaging to death?

'We're going to be late,' she repeated.

They weren't late, of course, but Cathy and Stuart had arrived ahead of them, and as Stuart's father opened the front door to them Abbie could see her daughter deep in conversation with her future mother-in-law, her face flushed as she refuted something the older woman was saying to her, causing Anne to purse her lips and shake her head. Both of them broke off their conversation as they saw that Abbie and Sam had arrived.

What, Abbie wondered uneasily, had their discussion—or argument—been about?

It was impossible for her to question Cathy on the subject as Anne was insisting on introducing both her and Sam to the evening's apparent guests of honour, a couple who were old friends of Stuart's parents but who had, it seemed, moved away from the area some years previously.

It was obvious that this couple—slightly older than Stuart's parents—had been very successful, and although privately Abbie found them almost unbearably smug she did her best to answer the volley of questions that Mary Chadwick fired at her.

Out of the corner of her eye she was aware of being watched by a solitary male guest whom she recognised as Anne's divorced cousin. She had been introduced to him at an earlier family gathering, although then he had had to leave early.

He was, Anne had been rather at pains to let her know later, something of the black sheep of the family, although she had not specified exactly what it was he had done to merit this title. Perhaps simply the fact that he was divorced was sufficient, Abbie had reflected cynically.

Now, as she managed to bring to an end Mary Chadwick's inquisitive questions and started to walk away from her and back to Sam, who was deep in conversation with Stuart's father, Anne's cousin intercepted her.

'We meet again. I hoped we would,' he told her, the humour in his eyes belying the triteness of his words.

'It must be fate,' Abbie quipped back drolly, welcoming the respite of a little light-heartedness after being cross-questioned by Anne's dearest and oldest friend.

'Fate giving a helping hand—or rather a hefty shove,'

he agreed, adding ruefully, 'You wouldn't believe how hard I've had to work on Cousin Anne to wangle an invite to this incredibly boring affair. She doesn't approve of me, you know. And I see she's already warned you against me—has she?' he queried, the amusement deepening in his eyes as Abbie inclined her head.

He was a very good-looking man, Abbie acknowledged, perhaps a year or so younger than her. Tall... although not quite so tall as Sam, nor quite so tautly muscled either. His expensive clothes cloaked what she suspected was the beginning of a slight paunch, although she also suspected that his vanity would never allow him to admit as much.

He was a man who quite obviously enjoyed flirting. A man who considered himself to be very much at home with and welcomed by her sex. But Abbie had met his type before, in several different guises. His insouciance amused her, and it was flattering to be singled out by him, but he was certainly not the type of man she could ever take seriously.

'Anne tells me that you and Cathy's father have recently been reconciled and are about to be remarried. Tell me it isn't true,' he demanded theatrically. 'Or let me persuade you that life might hold certain other interesting options,' he added outrageously.

'It isn't true,' Abbie told him judiciously, but although her voice was calm her eyes returned the flirtatious amusement she could see in his.

'I see...so there's hope for me, then, after all? Anne's a wonderful cook, you know,' he told her, his apparent change of subject causing Abbie to give him a puzzled look until he continued, 'Everyone says so, so it must be true. Can you cook?'

'Well enough,' Abbie agreed humorously, privately

reflecting on the cordon bleu diploma stuffed away in the deepest recesses of her desk.

'Wonderful. I'll let you prove it to me if you like—in the morning. I prefer a simple continental breakfast: fresh fruit juice, fresh fruit, warm fresh croissants, and a huge pot of real coffee. Breakfast in bed is such a sensual experience, don't you think? All those opportunities; all those deliciously warm, flaky crumbs of croissant; all those...'

Abbie couldn't help it; she burst out laughing and then stopped as she realised that those close enough to them had stopped talking whilst they eavesdropped on her and Anne's cousin's conversation.

As she turned her head to meet the disapproving glare of Mary Chadwick, to Abbie's own shock she heard herself saying, quite clearly, 'Breakfast in bed *is* a wonderful idea, but to thoroughly enjoy it the bed has to be properly dressed and the people in it must be...thoroughly *un*dressed...'

It was a stupid, idiotic, totally senseless thing to have said, of course, and she thoroughly deserved Cathy's angry denunciation of her, Abbie admitted to herself later in the evening.

After ignoring her all through the meal, once it was finally over Cathy followed her upstairs when Abbie went to collect the wrap she had worn over her suit, closing the bedroom door firmly as she followed Abbie inside, before demanding to know in a trembling voice just what her mother had thought she was doing.

'How could you embarrass me like that?' she asked bitterly. 'Behaving like that...flirting like that. Not just in front of Stuart's family but in front of Dad as well. I thought I knew you, Mum, but I'm beginning to think that I don't know you at all. Maybe, after all, Dad did have good reason to suspect that I wasn't his child,' she added unforgivably.

Abbie simply stood and stared at her. That Cathy was upset because she felt that Abbie had embarrassed her in front of Stuart and his family she could understand— even if she did think that Cathy was overreacting to what had, after all, been a relatively harmless piece of flirting—but to accuse her on the basis of that of having been unfaithful to Sam…

Neither of them heard the bedroom door open or realised that Sam had walked in until they both heard him saying roughly, 'Cathy, that's enough. I know you're upset, but that's no excuse for talking to your mother like that. What you just said to her was unforgivable.'

Both of them listened to him in mutual shock, Cathy recovering first to appeal to him, her voice trembling with anger and indignation, 'You saw her, Dad. You saw the way she behaved, the way she…made such a spectacle of herself, encouraging Anne's cousin to…to flirt with her like that.'

Over Cathy's head Sam's eyes met Abbie's, but she looked away quickly, unable to bear seeing the same angry contempt in his as she could see in Cathy's.

'How could you do it?' Cathy demanded, turning back to Abbie. 'How could you show me up, humiliate me like that, and in front of Stuart's parents…?'

Angry tears filled Cathy's eyes, but as Abbie stepped forward automatically to comfort her and apologise Cathy stepped quickly back from her, turning instead to Sam.

'I don't think I can ever forgive you for this,' she cried out theatrically.

It was Sam who stopped things going any further, saying quietly, 'That's enough, Cathy. I know you're upset but this isn't the time or the place.'

'But you must have felt the same as I did,' Cathy insisted passionately to Sam. 'You must have been just as embarrassed. After all, you and Mum *are* supposed to be reconciled, and yet she was openly flirting with another man—and in front of Stuart's parents as well—'

'No, Cathy, I did *not* feel embarrassed,' Sam interrupted her firmly.

And then, to Abbie's astonishment, he crossed the room and took hold of her hand, lifting it to his lips and kissing her fingers gently, looking right into her eyes as he softly told her...told *her*, Abbie acknowledged, and not Cathy, who was now standing watching them both in open-mouthed disbelief, 'You see, I have learned from my mistakes, and the worst mistake I have ever made in my whole life was not to trust your mother, not to trust her love, *our* love. That mistake brought us both unbearable pain. It cost you a father and it cost me the woman I loved and the daughter I would have loved. It hurt your mother unbearably, unforgivably, and it caused the kind of misery and destruction I can never forgive myself for.

'I know better now. If your mother chooses to enliven a rather dull dinner party with a little bit of harmless verbal flirtation, then she has every right to do so, and neither you nor I, nor indeed anyone else, has the right to criticise her for it. Loving someone, really loving them, means trusting them as well. I *know* that the fact that your mother might choose to spend a harmless few minutes talking or even flirting with someone else cannot have the slightest effect on her relationship with me. Nor could it ever change my love for her. Nothing can change that. Nothing ever could and nothing ever will.'

As she heard the sincerity in his voice Abbie looked deep into Sam's eyes, searching for some sign that his words were simply another part of the pretence he was

enacting to preserve Cathy's happiness. But no matter
how hard she searched all she could see in the grave
gaze steadily meeting her fiercely defensive scrutiny was
a warmth, a surety, a message that made her forget not
just Cathy's furious anger with her but also the very fact
of Cathy's presence in the room with them.

'Sam…' she began uncertainly.

But Cathy had started speaking as well, and as Abbie
focused unhappily on her she said shamefacedly, 'I'm
sorry, Mum. Dad's quite right…I overreacted. It's just,
well, I suppose I wanted you to make a good impression
on Stuart's family, and—'

'Your mother doesn't need to worry about the impression she makes on others and neither do you,' Sam
butted in firmly. 'Stuart loves you as you are, Cathy…'

'Oh, yes, I know that,' Cathy agreed, and then looked
uncomfortable as she explained, 'It's just that with Stuart
and Mum falling out over…over me wanting to know
you… It matters to me, Mum, that the two of you get
on,' she appealed to Abbie. 'I love you and Stuart so
much, I don't want there to be… I want you both to love
and appreciate one another as I do…'

Abbie couldn't quite conceal her confusion or her relief. 'Is that what this is all about?' she demanded, shaking her head slightly. 'I thought you were cross with me
because I wasn't more like Stuart's mother. I thought
you felt I'd let you down by not being like her.'

'What?' Now it was Cathy's turn to look astonished.
'How on earth could you *think* that?' she protested. 'You
must *know* that you are the most wonderful, precious
mother anyone could ever have,' Cathy told her emotionally. 'It just hurt me so much that you and Stuart
couldn't seem to get along, especially when I know how
special both of you really are. I just wanted Stuart to see
you as you really are, and for you to understand that

when he got in touch with Dad he wasn't doing it to get at you. He just wanted to do it for me...because he thought it would make me happy.'

'Oh, Cathy,' Abbie choked, hugging her and then releasing her to tell her firmly, 'You're right, he is a very special person, and I *haven't* appreciated him properly—but I promise you that from now on I shall do, and I promise you as well that I won't embarrass you by flirting any more,' she added generously.

'Well, you can flirt,' Cathy laughed, 'but only if it's with Dad—and I'd better go,' she added. 'Stuart will be wondering where on earth I am...'

'Well, we're leaving now too,' Sam told her as she went towards the door and opened it. 'We'll see you tomorrow.'

Abbie barely waited for Cathy to close the door behind her before turning back to Sam and demanding, 'Sam...?'

But once again she wasn't allowed to finish what she wanted to say, because Sam had taken hold of both her hands and had placed them gently against his chest, where he held them prisoner, covered by the warmth of his, and looked down into her eyes.

'I meant what I said, you know, about loving you...' he told her huskily.

'That... that can't be true,' Abbie protested shakily.

'But it is,' Sam assured her. 'Maybe this isn't the time to tell you this, but it has always been and it always will be true. I loved you all those years ago, when we were young, all the empty years in between, when we were apart—and I love you now. Why do you think I came back?'

'To see Cathy,' Abbie told him huskily.

'To see Cathy,' he agreed, 'and because of you. Surely you *must* have known?' he challenged her softly.

'Guessed how I felt when I touched you, when we made love...?'

'I thought it was just sex,' Abbie admitted painfully.

'Just sex?' Sam demanded self-mockingly. 'Oh, Abbie...'

'You said you would make sacrifices...for Cathy, and I thought...'

'You thought that taking you to bed was one of them. Was that the way it was for you?' Sam asked her softly.

His hands were no longer imprisoning hers, but now, for some odd reason, they seemed quite happy to cling possessively to his chest, whilst his were cupping her face, smoothing her skin, drawing her nearer so that the small tremors his earlier touch had evoked, and which she had thought she had fully under control, had become openly visible, sensual shudders of response to his nearness.

It was impossible for her not to look at his mouth and, having done so, even more impossible for her not to close the final distance between them with a small sound somewhere between a sigh and a plea, her face lifting automatically towards his, her lips parting.

'Abbie, Abbie, I love you so much, and I'm tired of playing the coward, being afraid to risk losing what little bit of you I have by admitting to you how I feel. This charade of our wanting to resurrect our love is no charade for me. I can't expect you to forgive me, and I certainly don't expect you to forget the past, nor to put either Cathy's or my needs and emotional desires above your own, and if it is just the rekindled flames of the physical passion we once shared that makes you respond so heart-achingly in my arms then you must tell me so, because physical desire alone will never be enough for me...'

'Not for me either,' Abbie admitted shakily. 'I...that

was why… I thought that was the way it was for you…just…just a physical…'

She tried to protest as he started kissing her, reminding him that they were in someone else's home and could all too easily be interrupted by other departing guests coming in search of their coats, but the sensation of his mouth moving against hers, the passionate, intense thrust of his tongue, the knowledge that the desire she could feel in him was born of love and not lust, made it impossible for her to resist him for very long, and it was several minutes before she could tell him huskily, 'Sam, I love you so much. How could I ever have let you go? How did I ever live all those years without you?'

'It was my fault.' Sam checked her soberly. 'Mine and—'

'No, we were both to blame,' Abbie interrupted him firmly. 'We both made mistakes.'

'Oh, Abbie, I don't deserve such generosity,' Sam protested gruffly as he took her back in his arms, and as she lifted her head to look at him Abbie could see the faint sheen of tears in his eyes.

'Oh, Sam,' she whispered emotionally.

'Oh, Abbie,' he returned, lifting the hand she had raised to his damp face to his lips and asking her, 'Will you think it unmanly of me if I tell you that these are far from being the first or only tears I've cried over you? Over you and for you—whilst I've lain in bed at night aching for you, cursing myself, wishing to hell I could turn back the clock and rewind time. I warn you now, Abbie, this time it's for ever, for eternity, infinity…for life and beyond life.'

'Yes,' Abbie agreed as she lifted her face for his kiss. 'Yes, yes. Oh, yes, Sam. Yes…'

'Let's get out of here,' Sam suggested fiercely as he

bent his head to kiss her. 'There are *some* things, *some* vows I may only want to make in private…preferably somewhere in the kind of privacy which includes a bed…an extremely large bed. Things which could, if we're lucky, take a long time to say and do…an extremely long time,' he added meaningfully.

Abbie laughed and whispered back appreciatively, 'I know the very place…'

'And tomorrow morning when you wake up in my arms there won't be any going back…any rejection of one another, any refusal to accept my love?' Sam asked her.

'No,' Abbie confirmed, her heart in her eyes as she looked at him quietly and confidently. 'You said that we can't forget the past, Sam, but we can use it to build our future together; we can use the mistakes we both made to build ourselves a stronger future and a stronger love. We can't forget the past but we can learn from it.

'Let's go home,' Sam breathed, his eyes dark with the emotions he was feeling.

'Yes,' she agreed softly, 'let's go home.'

As Sam held her in his arms Abbie knew that this time when they made love there would be no holding back, no fear within her of expressing and revealing her feelings, no need for either of them to hide from one another what they really felt.

EPILOGUE

'JUST look at Mum and Dad,' Cathy protested affectionately to her new husband. 'Anyone would think *they* were the ones who had just got married and not us.'

'Well, they have only been married for six weeks,' Stuart pointed out to her as they both turned to watch Abbie and Sam as they shared a lingering kiss.

'Mmm...that was nice,' Sam murmured appreciatively as he nuzzled the creamy warmth of Abbie's throat.

He laughed as she gently pushed him away, reminding him, 'This *is* our daughter's wedding day, remember...'

'Mmm...and officially you and I have still not had our own honeymoon,' he pointed out in return.

They had decided to wait until after Cathy was married before leaving for a two-month tour of Australia.

Sam wanted Abbie to see the land that had been his home in the years they had been apart, and there were certain things he needed to do, certain ends to be tied up, before he took up his post as Senior Chair at the university.

Abbie would have been quite happy for them to delay their own wedding until after Cathy had been married; they had, after all, been living together ever since the day they had declared their love for one another. But Sam had told her very firmly that he wanted the security of knowing that they were married. So they had very quietly, but very lovingly, been remarried in a small ceremony to which they had invited only close family and friends.

Cathy's wedding had been a very different affair.

Abbie had been amazed when she'd discovered how much the hotel she remembered as such a romantic location had altered since Sam had brought her there for their first night together. He had booked the same tower suite for them when they had visited the hotel, prior to Cathy's wedding, to make arrangements for the reception, but—and privately both Abbie and Sam had agreed—the place was just not the same.

The hotel was much larger now, with conference and leisure facilities, and it was making an ideal venue for a wedding reception.

As Sam took hold of her hand and they went to rejoin the others she smiled lovingly up at him. So much had changed since he had brought her here as a nervously excited virgin, and yet, in some ways, so little.

Their love, the love she had thought had been destroyed for ever, had proved so wonderfully strong and steadfast. As she looked across at Cathy, so radiantly happy as she stood next to Stuart, Abbie made a small prayer that their love would prove equally strong.

'You feel so afraid for them, don't you?' Stuart's mother whispered emotionally at her side. 'So afraid, and yet at the same time so…so humble. It makes you remember…' She paused and looked across at her own husband.

'Yes, it does,' Abbie agreed gently.

She and Stuart's mother had become if not close friends then at least good allies. After talking things over with Sam, Abbie had taken her courage in both hands and gone round to see and talk with Stuart's mother. The resulting conversation had done a good deal to clear the air, and Anne had admitted to her what Sam had already suggested—that she had felt envious and over-

awed by Abbie because of her achievements in the outside world.

They knew each other much better now, and when the
time came, as Abbie sincerely hoped it would, when they
both held in trust the special gift of loving their mutual
grandchildren the additional bond between them would
be one they both valued. They would be allies in that
love and not antagonists.

Abbie's smile broadened. Tonight, when they lay in
one another's arms in the privacy of their bedroom, she
would tell Sam again how much she loved him, how
much she valued this second chance they had been given
to share their love. And he would tell her the same thing,
both with and without words.

And their daughter, if she'd only known of the intense
physical passion that existed between them, would, no
doubt, have been both surprised and slightly shocked.

Abbie smiled a secret little smile to herself. There
were, after all, some things that Cathy, for all her apparent maturity, was still too young to know... Some
things, some pleasures she would, if life was as generous
as it had been to her mother, be allowed to discover for
herself.

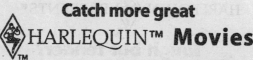

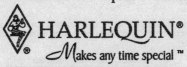

SEXY, POWERFUL MEN NEED EXTRAORDINARY WOMEN WHEN THEY'RE

Destined for Love

Take a walk on the wild side this October
when three bestselling authors weave wondrous stories
about heroines who use their extraspecial abilities to
achieve the magic and wonder of love!

HATFIELD AND McCOY
by HEATHER GRAHAM POZZESSERE

LIGHTNING STRIKES
by KATHLEEN KORBEL

MYSTERY LOVER
by ANNETTE BROADRICK

Available October 1998
wherever Harlequin and Silhouette books are sold.

HARLEQUIN®
Makes any time special ™

Silhouette®

Look us up on-line at: http://www.romance.net   PSBR1098

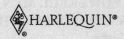 **HARLEQUIN**®

Not The Same Old Story!

 **HARLEQUIN ◇ PRESENTS**®

Exciting, glamorous romance stories that take readers around the world.

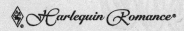 *Harlequin Romance*®

Sparkling, fresh and tender love stories that bring you pure romance.

 **HARLEQUIN**® *Temptation*

Bold and adventurous—Temptation is strong women, bad boys, great sex!

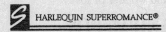 **HARLEQUIN SUPERROMANCE**®

Provocative and realistic stories that celebrate life and love.

 **HARLEQUIN**® **AMERICAN ◇ ROMANCE**®

Contemporary fairy tales—where anything is possible and where dreams come true.

 **HARLEQUIN**® **INTRIGUE**®

Heart-stopping, suspenseful adventures that combine the best of romance and mystery.

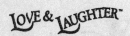 *LOVE & LAUGHTER*™

Humorous and romantic stories that capture the lighter side of love.

Mysterious, sexy, sizzling...

THE AUSTRALIANS

Stories of romance Australian-style, guaranteed to
fulfill that sense of adventure!

This November look for

Borrowed—One Bride

by **Trisha David**

Beth Lister is surprised when Kell Hallam kidnaps her on her
wedding day and takes her to his dusty ranch, Coolbuma. Just
who is Kell, and what is his mysterious plan? But Beth is even
more surprised when passion begins to rise between her and
her captor!

*The Wonder from Down Under: where spirited women win
the hearts of Australia's most independent men!*

Available November 1998
where books are sold.

HARLEQUIN®
Makes any time special ™